# FREUD AND
## GO SUR

Bill Green was born in Swan Hill, Victoria. A journalist and former Press Secretary for Jim Cairns, he now lives in Camperdown, Victoria, where he breeds race-horses when he is not writing. His published work includes the novels, *Small Town Rising*, Macmillan, 1981; and *Born Before the Wind*, Rigby, 1984.

# FREUD AND THE NAZIS GO SURFING

Bill Green

**Pan Books** Sydney and London

First published 1986 by Pan Books (Australia) Pty Limited
68 Moncur Street, Woollahra, Sydney
9 8 7 6 5 4 3 2
© Bill Green
Green, Bill, 1940–
Freud and the Nazis go surfing.
ISBN 0 330 27063 X (pbk.).
I. Title.
A823'.3
This book is sold subject to the condition that it
shall not, by way of trade or otherwise, be lent, re-sold,
hired out or otherwise circulated without the publisher's prior
consent in any form of binding or cover other than that in which
it is published and without a similar condition including this
condition being imposed on the subsequent purchaser.

Printed and bound in Australia by
The Book Printer, Maryborough, Victoria

*The author wishes to acknowledge the support given him by the Literature Board of the Australia Council.*

*For Andrew and Ben*

They met in a bar and he was explaining
how 'Baa, Baa, Black Sheep!' is about pubic hair
and how the clitoris is only really
the little boy who lived down the lane.

GAVIN EWART

I approach literary creation from a perspective which
treats it not as an irrational and mysterious phenomenon
... but on the contrary as a particularly precise and
coherent expression of the problems which pose themselves
to ordinary men in their daily lives and the ways in
which they are led to resolve them.

LUCIEN GOLDMANN

# CHAPTER 1

The heat was extraordinary that summer. It moved across those bright ocean days like a basting brush. Suddenly you had to shift from the glare to the shade. People walked over the sand in the haze from the heavily breaking waves as if they had changed worlds and were passively awaiting events beside a primaeval sea.

The country was still under the delusion that having survived a war it could survive anything. Men and women who had not been directly touched by war were growing up believing in heroism. It was the end of 1954 and I had been born a year before the war started. Nobody told me when it had begun, nor when it had finished. How the news was kept from me I'll never know. We lived on a property close to the Murray river, in virtual isolation. My parents who were pacifists had thought I should grow up without the knowledge that the countries of the world were prepared to annihilate one another. It gave them a feeling of superiority to know that they were protecting innocence from the horrors of the world. In their minds they were contributing somehow to a remedy for the prevailing evils. But in my mind it created a mystery to be fathomed only by intuition and outrageous behaviour, so that I sometimes wondered if my confusion wasn't in fact some form of insanity. The generation born during the turmoils of war seemed to have usurped all the savagery that had ever existed.

It was by the ocean that I began to suspect the extent of my own violence. After an evening meal at the guest house I went outside to climb the sand dunes. As I pushed through the ti-tree a small branch slapped me across the forehead. I turned on that tree in a rage, smashing it, mulching it underfoot. And then I turned on the next, the next and the next. Recovering, I saw the damage I had left behind me and burst into tears. I walked from the dunes and into the ocean. It was wondrous; there was such strength in the waves. They hurled me around without effort, as if I hardly existed, and I was soon completely recovered. I left the water knowing that people and the horrors they were carrying were ultimately nothing. I knew also that I would have to break future confusions down to their basic components and roll them in a prospector's dish for any gleams of gold.

I took tremendous risks in the ocean and was amazed myself by the things I could do with my strength. On a dumping wave ten feet high a quick butterfly stroke would have me forward of the break and the rush of white water, and I would cleave the surface like a bouncing keel. Several times I was forced down close to the sand ripples, only to be catapulted above the waves like a lost board.

My bursts of loutish behaviour didn't go unnoticed around the guest house. My remarks to passers-by in the halls and dining-room became cynical. It wasn't the whimsical cynicism of the defeated, but a crackle from the surgings of doubt. Hearing my ravings people would emit weak bleats of laughter, not immediately believing what they heard. They would focus on the elaborate dried flower arrangements in the halls as they passed me.

My parents were cool for a while but then they let me know that my behaviour rubbed them raw. They packed me off to boarding school when I was ten years old; by then my constant abrasiveness had become a source of marital disruption.

A farmer reacts to suffering with violence. At first he keeps it well suppressed, but it will break through and he'll grab an animal and kill it. I had seen my father kill stock with his bare hands, and I hadn't thought twice about it. I had learned to hunt and kill as a child when I wandered down the still creeks that lay in a web across our country. To watch violence performed can be a quite ordinary experience: a perfunctory blow to the brain shell and something that was, is no longer. I could take that. But my father couldn't. He couldn't forgive himself for outbreaks of useless savagery. He repressed his guilt by advising us that nobody was guilty of anything: you try to behave according to the best attitudes, but if you stray it's not really your own fault — external circumstances are such that you can't outmanoeuvre them. On a daily basis he convinced himself that pacifism was the correct attitude.

One morning at the guest house I told my mother I wouldn't mind fucking a particular friend of hers. She loosed the old man at me. He made a choking sound as he pushed me towards the door, and kicked my arse as he followed me onto the verandah. I turned to meet him as he came through the verandah door. He weighed fourteen stone and I neatly put my shoulder in his stomach and hung him over my back. I ran to the hallway with him, letting him bounce. I placed him, standing, next to one of the dried flower arrangements. He laughed from his ungainly position at a woman guest who was passing through to the black-tiled showers, sand clinging to the backs of her thighs. He was quick though.

'Never dare your children to do anything,' he said in answer to her smile. 'It can be dangerous.'

He was an articulate bastard for a farmer: he had been living for so long with a squeeze, a pressure, which had forced him into introspection. I recognised that he saw something of himself in me.

Leaving my father in the hall I went to my room to get my bathers and towel for the beach. I didn't know why I had informed my mother of my lusts for her friend. The image of the woman in a wispy cocktail dress had come to me only the instant I said I wanted to fuck her (I had never fucked anything but my looped fingers), and even though the outburst had astounded me I didn't want to take it back. I knew instinctively that such rashness was part of my development, although I didn't properly understand it. With all the conviction of naivety, I reasoned that truth had been the motive for my outburst. And I decided then that I wanted to begin telling people my truths; others had heaped enough of theirs on me.

My parents had never wanted to know a great deal about me. It had taken a bank loan to send me to school, which meant they had energetically planned not to have me around. Newtown College was a second-class school as boarding schools go, and I hated the hypocrisy and pretentiousness of the place. I was sent to a second-class school because my parents hadn't thought me too bright and didn't want to waste their money on what they regarded as a first-class school.

But then a few weird things occurred that made my parents regard me with some awe. Several of the masters began to consider that I was very bright. In my mind there was no evidence of this. I knew that if I was bright there were plenty I had met who were brighter. It was just that up the bush there was no one to listen to them. They usually earned themselves the title of local character — that way people could forget them. I had no illusions about the supposed benefits of being bright. I resented the title they were attempting to impose on me.

On the beach one day, my mind dozing in the sun, it slowly became clear to me that I was intimidated by the house guests. Over the three years we had stayed at Debonair my parents' friends had grown used to treating me with condescension. They drifted through the summer days with such glib greetings and happy smiles that it seemed as if they were trying very hard to say nothing at all to each other.

I decided that if I was to enjoy this summer I would need to make an effort at seeing the guests in the context of their respective backgrounds. A similar challenge had occurred during my first year at school: the kids I was with came from the large bluestone homes of the Western District graziers, where the social system supported the image those kids had of themselves. No such system existed in the Riverina. Kids from there had to find their own reference points. The Western District social system had evolved because the graziers were imitative and hoped their children would in turn imitate their attempts at being English aristocrats. They turned a blind eye to their own traditions, rejecting the excess of grubby bloodshed there. They wanted to distance themselves from the way their ancestors had acquired the land. American racists were babes-in-arms compared with the Australian squatters and their dealings with the blacks.

This summer Debonair housed disparate couples. My parents were holidaying as always with their friends Judge Ralph Lurie and his wife Sarah. They had gone to school together, university together, married in the same flush of romance, and the men had been each other's best man. It was a phoney mateship, each of them careful to protect the self-regard of the other.

There was the insurance salesman, Arthur Waterhouse and his wife Lynette, who had arrived in a borrowed Jaguar. He'd been suspiciously forthcoming about that. Arthur was a sharp dresser with very short hair. He was athletic and wore clothes that could have been American. His tennis hat was sharply peaked. His wife was enthusiastically younger than the other wives at the guest house, and she seemed to presume that this gave her special advantages. She called the judge Ralph.

On the beach, three girls broke my reverie. They rushed past, spraying sand over my oiled skin. I was pissed off at the intrusion until I saw that they looked about my age. The beach was marvellous: so much colour, and the girls threading their way swiftly through the crowd. One of the girls moved more gracefully than the others, her legs slim and pliant and her waist tiny from the curve of her hips. It was as if an inner astuteness had moulded a quick body. Mostly by the time such girls reach my age they're spoilt rotten with special attention. I'd seen girls of that type going out with my older cousins; they wanted sports cars and blokes that constantly praised their physical attributes. They destroyed the maturity of a roomfull of adults within seconds of entering it. Their smiles were devastating. I lay back as the three of them ran into the surf.

With the exception of my father, everyone at the guest house was slightly in awe of Squadron Leader Long and his wife Judith. In private my father spoke of the incompetence of the Royal Australian Air Force. He said the government had to stop them looking for submarines off the coast during war-time because every aircraft that motored off from the coast failed to reappear. They didn't fight submarines, or even during the entire war find any — they just lost themselves. This outrageous story of my father's, which I didn't for a moment believe, was later supported by official histories. In New Guinea, my father claimed, they invented a bomb that blew off the tails of the bombers that dropped them. It took them some time to discover this unique ability, for the bombers didn't return.

My father told these stories so that he wouldn't have to compete with a war hero. It made no difference to my mother; the Squadron Leader might personally have saved her from the rampant Japanese. He wasn't too bad a bastard, full of winks and nods. During the pre-dinner drinks in my parents' room, my father would hold the bottle out as if to look at the golden light there, and the Squadron Leader, knowing it was a gesture directed at his drinking, would give me an accomplice's wink.

I had difficulty working out the Jewess and her German husband. Rachel was beautiful; on the way to her morning shower she would stride down the hallways in a flowing dressing-gown. Her laugh was high and shiny and sometimes, if prolonged, it would end in dreadful sobs. She had been a prisoner of war and had shown everyone at pre-dinner drinks her tattooed numbers. Or rather they had asked and she had shown. My mother would have liked not to believe her stories, but they were well documented and she couldn't express disapproval.

On the beach the sun gave the illusion that everybody understood everything and had lived and suffered equally. Responses were slowed and graceful, twitches and stutters could be repressed simply by a glance at the rolling ocean, and everybody was prepared to lose themselves in the conventional beauty of their surroundings. It was a dangerous illusion; people mistook one another. An individual on holiday is different from one at work or in a routine. At first I thought simply that Rachel was different because she lived as if on a permanent holiday. But then, lying awake listening to her sobbing fill the guest house at night, I realised that living would always be full time effort for her. I began speculation on the German husband but his function led me only to images of sexual cruelty and that led nowhere: I was on her side not his.

Late that morning I saw the girl again. I examined her closely. When she stood next to a lifesaver I noted how tanned and tall she was, and how she stood with her legs slightly apart. She was laughing a lot, her dark hair swaying back from her face, so I pompously labelled her as spoilt and incapable of serious conversation or contemplation. I noticed too that when she was relaxing, lying back, face to the sun, one leg slightly bent, she would start occasionally and look at her watch. When she left the beach I followed her. She was working in the large Kings cafe with the rest of the final year students from one of the city high schools. There was a group at the Kings every summer enjoying a working holiday while they waited for their examination results to appear in the papers. They did shift work and slept in the huge corrugated iron shed behind the cafe. The girls' digs were separated from the boys' by a hanging hessian wall. Their obvious camaraderie and their ability to make money while having a holiday made me feel distinctly deprived.

Several mornings later, I spoke to the girl when we passed on the dunes. I was heading for the early morning surf and she was leaving.

'Good is it?' I asked with a smile.

'Freezing,' she said without looking at me, and walked on nonchantly.

'It'll be a relief then,' I called over my shoulder.

'Definitely,' she replied without looking back.

I was ridiculously elated. My boarding school days were going to be only a dim memory. Taking initiative would give me joy, and counterbalance the fear engendered under a regimented and unimaginative system.

In the evening I laid siege to the Kings. It was a cavernous building; even the long counter appeared diminished in the huge space. There was a juke box down one end near the stand with the westerns and the comics, and in front of that, yet still beyond the counter, were tilted boxes of fruit and shelves for the bread. The floor was smooth cement and the freezer where the icecreams and the milkshakes were served was gleaming silver, polished daily by one of the students.

I hung around the western stand watching the girl. She was capable, and could do several tasks at once, like taking payment from the counter while leaning back to remove the milkshake container from the machine. I watched as one of the boys attempted to emulate her style. He grabbed at the container without really holding it and it dropped as the mixing blade sliced his thumb. He turned his thumb upwards; the blood welled from the slit and ran down his wrist. She caught the blood in some newspaper and steered the boy through the swinging doors to what I assumed was a rear bathroom or basin. Watching her face I could see there was no real concern, and that her action was prompted by knowledge and ability.

So I thought briefly about the notion of ability, as I looked at the cover of a Zane Grey western: people generally only do the things they are sure they can do; faced with a problem they act according to their abilities and not in the way they should act — or so I concluded to myself and Zane Grey. On the the other hand, I, who had no skills, was prepared to act in any way at all, but had no idea how to start.

When the girl returned I managed to meet her eyes without flinching. I had read a magazine article on how to relate to true beauty in the opposite sex and it meant gazing at a photograph of a woman who conformed to your standard of beauty until you were at ease with it. Having masturbated before many such photographs I found that the advice was inadequate, actually fraudulent. I nodded to the girl as I approached her section of the counter.

'Did you swim again today?' I asked.
'What?'
'I saw you this morning at the beach.'

'Oh.'

'Are you free after work?'

'Sorry,' she said. 'I don't go out with surfers.'

'That's good,' I said. 'I'm not one.'

'You're not in the surf club?'

'No. They're a soft lot.'

'They're fresh,' she said. 'And keen on themselves.'

'That's not me,' I said. 'I'm a very hesitant person.'

She laughed. 'You don't sound like it.'

'That's only because I'm a bit of a bullshit artist sometimes, although I'm pretty serious mostly.'

How could she refuse me? There was a broad spectrum of appeal there despite none of it being remotely like me. Conning sheilas wasn't that hard after all. And last year at school I had contemplated blowing my tool off with a shotgun. Marvellous how things changed.

'No,' she said mockingly. 'You don't say.'

I laughed, showing all my teeth.

'I'd really like to take you out. I mean even if there's another bloke.'

I could see immediately that I would have welcomed there being another bloke. It would make for challenge and intrigue. I thought how ridiculous I was.

'Sorry,' she said. 'Would you like anything while you're here? Another milkshake?'

I shook my head.

She moved away to serve another customer, but smiled back over her shoulder. It may have been an ordinary smile for her, but I read it as entirely welcoming. It wasn't a flirtatious smile; but then some women haven't any idea of the dynamite effect a broad smile can have, especially if it's received by a person who is not used to being smiled at.

I walked out of the cafe feeling pretty good. I had taken a step away from my adolescent fumblings. The evening was coming down quickly and the sand dunes across the road were silhouetted against the gold of a sunset. The air was warm.

Anglecrest was a holiday town. On its best days a big surf ran there, and the waves rolled for a good hundred metres after breaking. On its worst days the waves could still be ridden. The formation of the beach prevented a chop except when the big run-outs developed on a tide change.

Over the Christmas break the population of the town swelled from around five hundred local residents to about three thousand. The town nestled around the beach, hidden from the really strong north winds of summer by the foothills of the Otway ranges. It was a lively little town, although until this year I hadn't realised it. Only now, at sixteen, was I on the verge of being able to participate. As I walked up the hill to the guest house I felt that not even the guests could phase me any more.

On the verandah I ran into the adults filing into dinner. Usually they were boisterous after drinks, but there was some anger loose amongst them this evening. There were no laughs or jokes about jumping the queue.

'Evening judge,' I said boldly, confronting his haughtiness.

He had the eyes of a basking lizard, and his skin would eventually hang in paper-thin folds. His hair was slicked back like an ugly Valentino. It indicated the era when he had made a decision on how he would look for the rest of his life. His jaw this evening was thrust forward, his mouth pulled down into a petulant half moon. Others were attempting his depth of feeling. It pissed me off that everyone else deferred to him. The judge had nodded to me at my greeting, and lowered his eyes in surprise, or at least to cover his surprise. I defied them all with a smile. I had no idea where this capacity for careless and carefree greeting had arrived, but it was satisfying.

My parents were already seated when I walked in. The dining-room was panelled with dark wood and the tables covered with thick white cloths were bright and expectant. My mother drew her napkin from its ring and smiled tightly.

'What have you been doing today?' she asked.

'Nothing really. Swimming I s'pose.'

She had obviously abandoned any idea of taking me to task for my confessed lust. In fact there seemed to be a pact in the air.

'I hope you kept out of the sun. Your back is too burnt.'

'Yeah, I know. What happened this evening?'

I looked around at the various tables and saw how carefully nobody was looking at anybody.

'Been some arguments?'

'Not arguments really,' my mother said.

My father moved as if to stop any further conversation, but then he geared himself to attack his meal, taking his soup with tiny slurps. I think meals were a torture for him. He only ate as some sort of obligation to continue his life.

'What then?' I asked.

'There were some more discussions of the Petrov thing,' my father said.

'Who was on which side?' I asked, used to the diverse arguments and theories that surrounded the defection of the Russian spy.

'Which side was the judge on?'

'Not our side,' my father said a trifle bitterly. 'He thinks the country is running with commos, like sheep in a paddock.'

'What did you say to him?' I asked.

'That it was political, to make the Labor Party look bad.'

'And that's all?'

'There was some other discussion,' my mother said.

'Not worth going into,' my father said.

I looked at my father. He was munching bread, his jaw muscles taut with the effort.

He disliked my inclinations towards being a smart arse and I knew he felt that the faster he could finish his meal and get away from my presence the better. He wanted a son to whom he could relate. A person who could take over some of the running of the farm and who could joke his way through the day about the things that my father found amusing — which wasn't too much in my opinion. He wanted a mate. But like most bosses who want mates, he wanted to be the one who set the ground rules. My mother was a living apology for her failure to produce off-spring that weren't up to her husband's expectations.

'Rachel and Hans,' I asked. 'Which stance did they take?'

'They thought a spy like Petrov was a ridiculous figure. What could he possibly want in Australia? They thought all he could collect out here was a bag of old rubbish, so why did it have to begin a persecution of communists? They said it was just a little country wanting to have its own McCarthyism.'

I knew that wouldn't have pleased my father who wanted to take both Australia, and his own ideas and perceptions, seriously. Already he knew no one else did, but he thought there might be a higher court out there somewhere that would acknowledge his recognition of universal problems.

'You'll have to stop sucking around the judge then,' I said.

My mother's nails whispered over the surface of the table cloth.

'What do you mean by that?' she asked, her neck changing colour.

'I don't understand,' my father said, feigning tolerance.

He would begin to listen like that, and if there was

a later outburst he would always remember how calmly he had begun to reason my behaviour. But he was only fuelling the hurt that would then allow him to turn on me with no qualms. If people hurt him he retaliated, and the degree to which he had been hurt didn't matter; his response was always full blast. But now I thought, listen Dad, you've got to throw in a check on that rage because my strength is equal to yours. And I realised then that no one looking at this family group would even remotely understand the anger building up around the table. But then I wondered how many families themselves understood the processes involved in their own conflicts.

'It seems to me,' I began, 'that people in this guest house really look up to him.'

'He's a man of some vision,' my mother replied.

My father didn't say a word. His white-faced anger was enough.

Was I just testing myself, to observe how I coped with the presence of hostiles? I wasn't confronting the circumstances with any real courage. But it was clear that nothing of my past life of obedience was going to accompany me in my growing rebellion. And boarding school bullying had hardened me to concealed threats.

Rachel and Hans entered the dining-room late and they looked around the room with probing glances. I couldn't tell whether the others answered their looks. Rachel's hair filled the room with its movement. It was lush and glossy and her face would have been classically beautiful but for a twist of her lips that made it even more interesting. The twist seemed to infuse her full lips with an energy of their own. Hans looked sly, as always, as if he were getting away with something. Or was that simply the role others had projected on him?

They had a corner table close to the window next to the plum tree. The air through the open window carried the smell of salt from the ocean mixed with the smell of moving dust. There was something strange about the old plum tree. The heat had accelerated its decay. When Rachel caught my gaze she smiled back in a perfunctory way. I lowered my eyes. I didn't have to worry about blushing because the sun had burnt my skin bright red. Her faint smile had disturbed me. She was someone who could see through my callow motives. Hey, at least I'm trying I thought. Alright, so I wanted to know about her and Hans and how they got on in bed. My father had said he thought Hans must be a very understanding man, but I thought she was the one who understood. My face had begun to sweat. It made me feel uneasy, but then I saw that all the others who had been for pre-dinner drinks also had a sheen of sweat on their faces. The light through the stained glass insets in the dining-room door gave their faces a greenish tinge. Somebody out there had turned on the bright light above the ping-pong table.

Coffee was served in the games room. I headed for the great steaming urn and dashed back to my parents' friends, cups and saucers in hand, without spilling a drop. My generosity had a purpose: I wanted to keep everything calm. They smiled weakly at me.

For some of the guests it was going to be a long night to endure, with no relief from the heat. It was a world I liked. I was comfortable in hot weather. I had the ocean to refresh me if I wanted, and I'd sneak from my bed in the early hours after midnight and dare myself to enter the chill blackness. It was adventure. There could have been sharks cruising through the shallows at high tide. They'd be drawn by the heat in the same way I was. I had caught waves after midnight. I was somebody.

## CHAPTER 2

You've all noticed that odd type of character who hangs around in the sand dunes watching the beach and the sea. He usually turns up just before evening, and you say to yourself by Jesus that's some sort of pervert. You swing around to get a closer look at him, but he's gone.

I'd noticed this particular bloke several times before. He was a farmer. He wore khaki trousers and a navy blue shearer's singlet. In those days farmers who lived near the sea didn't make much use of it. They could live five miles from the beach and if their road to town didn't take them along the coast they'd only see it once or twice a year. So it was unusual for someone like him to be standing on a high dune looking down. From a distance you noticed his arms. They were like two hams hanging and they seemed thick as his body. Passing him on a track I had to move aside to avoid his bulk. His eyes stared through you blankly. It wasn't that you remembered him later, or even thought about him, it was just that when you saw him again you thought, boy that bastard is dangerous, how could he have slipped my mind? I knew he was quick on his feet, though I couldn't work out why, until I remembered that he wore sand shoes. I watched him once when the sand began to slide beneath him on a steep dune; he took quick, effortless steps to keep his balance. He had the beginnings of a beer gut but it didn't hinder his mobility.

I began to meet Gillian Blyton on the beach whenever she wasn't on duty. After our brief conversation over the counter at the Kings I felt I could approach her with more confidence. I bumped into her one morning in the surf.

I was out behind the waves, bullshitting with some of the junior kids from the surf club, when I saw her wander down from the dunes, drop her towel and enter the water. Her wisp of a body was unmistakable. She stood for a moment pinning back her hair. Her legs were wide apart, and with her arms up her body looked like a tensed bow. I caught the next wave in, and with my head up watching her, my body high and humped on the break, I steered towards her. When the wave dropped me in waist-deep water I let my body ease slowly forward until I bumped her thigh with my head. She had obviously waited for me to do it. There'd been plenty of time for her to avoid me.

'I knew it was you,' she said.

I stood up grinning, tossing the water from my face and hair. Our bodies were very close, but she stepped back and looked up at me without intimidation.

If she started work in the afternoons I'd sometimes walk around to the garage in the late morning and find her lying on her camp-stretcher, reading. I'd sit down a couple of stretchers away. Or if she was sunbaking on the lawn, I'd sit with my back to the wall of the garage. She seemed to have a moat around her. She needed at least a couple of metres between us. If I trespassed on that space she'd move away or sit up suddenly and hug her knees. Instinctively I began wearing more clothes when I was around her. Instead of only bathers, and a towel over my shoulder, I'd wear an Aertex shirt and shorts. She was much easier then. And she relaxed progressively as our conversations became more intimate.

After a few days, she began talking about herself. She was born in Sydney, but after her parents died in a car accident when she was eight she went to live with her aunt in Melbourne. When she had saved enough money working at the Kings, she would head back to Sydney to stay with friends until university started. She couldn't wait to get to Sydney's summer beaches.

'And you,' she asked, 'are you going to pass?'

'Sure,' I said. I had travelled well through all my exam papers.

'But I don't think my schooling is going to do me much good. It was all bullshit.'

I had known there was no escape from the system, and although I had performed my work with mischievous abandon, I had been serious enough about getting a pass.

She began to laugh.

'What do you mean bullshit?'

'The stuff they taught us has no relation to anything we really wanted to know. Did any of it benefit you personally?'

'Not me. But some kids.'

'Bullshit. It was all tired bloody facts about a world they made dull for us.'

'You didn't have the teachers we had.'

'I'll prove I'm right,' I said. 'Can you honestly say a teacher ever told you anything worth knowing that you didn't already know?'

'Not for want of trying,' she said and began laughing: at first a chuckle, which must have released something secret and deeply amusing, because she started to laugh openly, deliciously. Delicious to watch anyway.

'God,' she said at last, lying back. 'I've spent some terrible years at study and now you tell me!'

I think that was when she decided she could enjoy my company. We picked up our towels and headed off to the beach for a quick dip before she started work. Climbing the dunes I watched sweat trickle over her dark skin to her backbone. It ran into her bathers. I wanted to know where it would finish. I'd never thought of sweat as clear moisture before. I touched her back once and she flinched slightly as if she didn't know what it meant, but then she smiled at me over her shoulder.

From across the sand Frank Gordon saw me and called out:

'Hey Traven aren't you in the club this year?'

I shook my head and waved my hands in a NO. He was about thirty metres away and didn't walk any closer.

'We could do with you in the boat again,' he called. I spread my towel on the sand.

'I thought you weren't in the surf club,' she accused.

'I'm not,' I said. 'It's a waste of time. I rowed with the junior crew last year. It was bloody boring after a week or two!'

She didn't comment but lay back on the sand. Her long legs were brown and I didn't mind if she caught me looking at them. When she tossed her head back to gaze at the moving ocean, I watched her lips. They had been deeply carmined and made the tan of her face quite gorgeous to look at. I wasn't sure she knew how good she was, although occasionally she would turn on her hip and let one inner thigh slap nicely against the other. The sight and sound almost released me from my hesitation and I could have run my hand around the edge of her bathers. I told myself I didn't know her at all, that this person who bewildered and fascinated me could be anyone. She could be entirely different from my fantasy of her. These thoughts, perhaps prompted by intuition, prevented me from making a move. I lay back and let the heat absorb me. I think she touched my hand while I was sleeping, but I may have dreamt it.

She woke me when she said, 'They're taking the boat out'. I looked up to see the surfboat wobbling down to the sea on rubber rollers. 'Yeah,' I answered and was asleep again. That dreamy state had me closer to her than any waking moment. I guessed it must be the intimacy of two people asleep.

Later she touched my arm gently and I was instantly awake.

'I've got to go,' she said. 'I'll see you later. I'll come down for the dinner break.'

I speculated on the change in our relationship. Her voice had been warmer, with a giving quality about it. And then I worked it out: she was no longer on the defensive. She had accepted something about me. I hoped it was not because I had gained in status by being a club member. My grandmother had once said you could always tell if someone was good or not by the kind of person who liked them. I wondered whether everybody made use of this yardstick. My grandmother liked people who were members of the Australia Club, although I don't think she knew many of them personally.

At lunchtime I strolled up to the guest house. My parents had been out with their friends on a morning walk along the cliffs to the south. From their demeanour it was obvious they would have liked to despatch some members of the walking party over the edge. They were not prepared to talk easily about the recent happenings.

'Your father couldn't convince Ralph that the government was over-reacting to the events of the past year. Your father thinks it's all a plan to put a lot of outspoken people in gaol.' Mum was goading the old man a bit. She didn't always do his talking for him. She wanted him to see the humour of it, to approach it all in a different way.

'He wouldn't take any notice of you,' I said, ' because he's a judge and you're a farmer. Judges are immune to the thought that anybody else can be right. I bet all the judges have the same opinion of the Petrov thing.'

'It seems everybody in the country has,' he said.

'No, the workers would be different,' I said.

My father had talked often of the working-class and for him they were always the heroes, although he didn't mix with many, except the hands on our farm, and he didn't think they were heroes. Just the opposite in fact.

It was me who liked being with them. The bastards had such a sly sense of humour, always taking the mickey out of the old man and me: you could piss yourself laughing over the smallest thing.

'Yes,' he said. 'The unions will see the thing through all right.'

'Unless the judge and his mates do first,' I said.

'He's not involved in that way,' he said.

It was peculiar the way my parents changed on holiday. Of course, they were among people unlike those they mixed and worked with the rest of the year. It was as if my father became another man. I was different too. My mother loved being on holidays, because she could sway easily between subtle and raucous humour and she was always very popular. She used to bait the old man, while completely respecting his ideas. But the Petrov thing was a bit of a challenge.

Prime Minister Menzies had been on the rampage. His backers were scared the workers and Communist sympathizers in the Labor movement would rise up. Menzies said the defecting spy had proof of everything. Well, that's what the newspapers claimed.

I was finishing my salmon salad when I said to my father that he couldn't be certain of anything about the judge.

'Why?' he asked.

'Well it's a bit like you,' I said. 'If people could see you operating around the farm they'd never take you for a pacifist, or any sort of thinker. I mean your ideas would even surprise the people you work with.'

My mother looked sharply at my father.

'I understand that,' Dad said.

'Same with the judge. Remember a couple of years ago he showed us all that stuff he'd collected from the war.'

'I do.'

'I bet he didn't show that to everybody. It was because you were talking about hunting and the way you enjoyed preparing all the things you ate. And then he said he had something to show you, and we looked at all those weird weapons. Daggers that had knuckle dusters, machine pistols, revolvers that had knives connected to the handle. And then those recruiting posters for the German army.'

'Hundreds of people have those sorts of collections,' my father said. 'There's a bloke at home who has the base of his light stand made out of a spent shell from some battleship, and a dozen other things.'

'That's right,' I said. 'People love all that war stuff. But the judge didn't fight. He didn't just happen to stumble on all those things. He set out to make up a collection. It was very satisfying to him.'

'I still don't see what you're getting at.'

'I just think it's strange. Somebody who loves that kind of thing so much can't be a real judge. He's got his mind on all that other stuff.'


Around five I thought of going up to the cafe to meet Gillian, but then I thought no, I'll play it cool, I'll meet her here. She came up while I was dozing and flicked her towel at me.

'Lazy bastard,' she said.

When the breeze sprung up we decided to take a dip. The beach wouldn't be comfortable much longer, though the waves were still rolling easily, not much more than five feet, and the surfing was easy. We only needed to lean into the humped crests for the ride back into the soup. Deciding we'd had enough, she beat me to the sand on the last wave and ran up to her towel, shaking her hair and squeezing it out over one shoulder. I bounced around behind her and I even tried a leap that finished with the first part of a diving pike, before I hit the sand.

By the time I got there she was looking away across the beach, holding her towel up to her eyes so that she seemed like some desert Arab. The farmer was there, standing on the ridge of a nearby dune. He was so still I would never have noticed him, as he blended in against the ti-tree. Gillian wasn't visibly shaking but her body was tense, as if she was frightened or trying to stop the shivers you get when you've been too long in the sea. She turned away to look at the water. I stood watching the bloke, hands on hips.

'Are you OK?' I asked her, without taking my eyes off the figure. 'Are you OK?' I asked again. She didn't reply. The bastard wasn't intimidated by my tough schoolboy act so I gave him a last challenging look and turned away.

'He's not such a nice bloke,' I said. 'Have you had trouble with him?'

'No.'

'Well he seems to have had some effect on you,' I said. The brisk wind was invigorating after the numbing chill of the water, and I began to feel protective and capable. 'Do you know someone like him?'

'No,' she said. 'Shut up will you.' I dried myself energetically with my towel. Even being silenced by a good-looking girl was better than being ignored by her. I looked up again and the farmer was gone. Gillian draped herself in her towel, from chin to knee.

'Let's go back around by the dunes,' she said as I made to climb.

'Down the end,' she added as she nodded towards the estuary.

'You really don't want to go near him do you?'

'No,' she answered with irritation.

We walked in silence to the banks of the river. It was closed off from the ocean here by sand fluffy as snowdrifts.

Back at the Kings she touched my arm. 'Thanks for not pestering me over that man.' I grinned at her.

'You'll probably tell me all about it,' I said.

'No, I don't think so.' She ran off into the garage to change before going back to work. I walked over the road and into the ti-tree. I wanted to know more about the bastard before he left the area.

From my first interest, at the age of eight, in couples making love, I had learned to move through ti-tree noiselessly. I could fly down the sandy tracks without a sound. Often I had surprised small snakes, and if their sensitive scales couldn't detect my approach, a man certainly couldn't. The farmer would be my victim here. I had often run from lovers taken by surprise, escaping effortlessly, although their struggles to get their clothes on and buttoned up gave me as much as forty yards start.

But the farmer was gone. I tracked through the dunes quickly and then had the strangest sensation that he was watching me. For him to disappear so completely from this area without me sighting him crossing the road or trotting along to the next beach was impossible. To vanish so perfectly meant that he was adopting the first rules of camouflage. That takes a special effort of will if you're a grown man. A quick stooping, or sliding into thick and untravelled parts of the bush here, makes you for a moment completely vulnerable, open to immediate suspicion as a lurker. That was a game you played knowing there could be consequences. The thought pulled me up short. I was in a narrow path cut through a dune that was covered with relatively deep-rooted grass. It was very quiet, a stupid place to be, for the dune was ten feet higher than I was and a perfect place for an ambush.

I kept still for quite a while, testing the patience of whoever was shadowing me. It's a trick children play when their parents keep shouting at them, while they try to work out what all the noise means. Usually they end up getting belted for it. I felt my heart beating faster and my breathing grow stronger, and I thought of the way a car can overheat when its engine has just been turned off. If the farmer was watching me, or saw me enter the cutting and not emerge, he would know I was initiating a change of rules, that I was attempting to become the stalker. I jumped to the top of the cutting with a running leap, digging my feet into the soft sand and grass roots, and then I crawled up further to examine the other side. Nothing. I wormed my way into the grass thinking: *if it wasn't that I liked the girl, I wouldn't be doing this*. But with my head and body close to the ground my perspective altered. The grass and sand, the minute grains, became important. The long blades curved away from their roots and then curved across the sky. But dallying like this can be deceptive, can distract you from the job at hand.

I began to be frightened. I needed to know more. I shouldn't be caught here by an animal like that farmer and have everything come to a sudden stop. On my elbows I slithered my way up to the top of the dune. I couldn't make the last few feet because the vegetation gave out completely. But I was close enough to watch the smaller dunes stretch away to Stingaray Point. In the evening light a distant belt of trees glistened, their leaves a metallic rippling. I was kidding myself. It could have hidden an army. Then I saw a figure emerge from the trees, momentarily silhouetted against the sand, and then he was gone. He must have been running, judging the speed with which he had leapt back into the treeline. I reasoned that he hadn't had to show himself. There'd been nothing to make him break cover. I took a line across the belt of trees to where I thought he might emerge. A small gravel road met the metal road. The sun was still on the slope of dune where I lay, so I moved down cautiously to drop into the cutting, and then hared off towards the gravel track. But halfway there I changed my mind and crossed the metal road into a paddock with trees along its fence line.

A few minutes later I watched the farmer cross the road onto the track. He kept looking back into the ti-tree as if he expected someone, — me? It made me laugh, a shade nervously. He began to walk briskly. I started to jog; I was about two hundred yards in front of him and kept to the trees hoping the light would hold out so I could keep up the pace. Then he broke into a run. He ran as if he were charging out onto a footy oval at the start of a match — shoulders back, his stride exaggerated. And he was fit. I thought: *this silly bastard is running from me,* and giggled at the inanity of it all.

I almost lost him when he took a path off the track. Instantly he was swallowed by the thick bush. I crossed, thinking *well, I'm in this now* and began to lope silently along the grey sand track. I'm not sure how far we travelled but I stopped when I heard the scrape of a shed door somewhere in front of me. It was a definite dragging sound. I heard a car back on the gravel, so we were probably no more than a mile in, though there was a stillness to the stunted forest that resembled complete isolation.

I left the path and circled, catching a glimpse of a corrugated iron shed, rusted, and crooked with subsidence. There were signs of considerable activity here. The area was cleared of all undergrowth and the grey sand was as pockmarked as a beach after a hot day. There was deep scarring of the sand around several of the larger trees, which surprised me. The place was like a two-up area, and I'd seen lots. Near any small town on the Murray river — and that's where our property was — there were little clearings like this just over the border in New South Wales. Two-up games could be conducted without interference from that state's police because the towns on their side of the river were usually several hundred miles away and any attempted police raid would be spotted by sympathetic farmers all along the route. Usually the clearings were close to aboriginal camps and the women there would be visited by anyone with the money for a fuck when the game finished. This clearing was therefore unexpected. This was holiday country, and people weren't so desperate in these parts.

But then I saw ropes looped and trussed and swung up into the low branches of the trees. Fuckin' strange. I kept circling, well hidden by the undergrowth. I had no real conviction that he was busy in the shed and not looking for me. Continual movement was better.

I heard the sound of quick movements from the shed, and then soft thuds as if bags of wheat were being dropped from shoulder to earth. This was followed by cursings and more thumpings. Knowing now where the bastard was I stopped with the door of the shed clearly in view. He emerged shortly after, closing the door and padlocking it. He was hot and dirty and wiped his brow with the back of a meaty forearm. The heat in the iron shed must have been intense. Without another look he trotted off down the soft track and his footsteps were inaudible as soon as he turned out of view thirty yards on. I gave him around fifteen minutes to get well clear. As the scrubby forest grew darker I moved to the stack of fence posts leaning against the shed. They were newly cut — so there was to be fencing. I took a post, drove it into the door, and the lock was wrenched away. The crash was massive, so I walked back to the edge of the undergrowth. The smell from the shed was fecund, a musky animal smell, like the whiff of damp fox fur on a wet morning. From the bushes I watched the blackness of the open doorway. Nothing emerged. Then an almost imperceptible sound of breathing reached me. Occasionally it was a strained rasping.

I reckoned on enough time for an investigation by a cautious listener and crossed the clearing back to the shed. I pushed the door wide open and the sound of breathing stopped. It couldn't have been a dog, which, even if it was too frightened to bark, would still have leapt around me. This is bloody ridiculous, I thought; it won't be a ferocious animal — there are so few in Australia anyway. I stepped inside the door and stood to one side, my back against the wall. I could hear a peculiar sound, and then I realised it was only the rushing of blood close to my eardrums. The smell was strong, like when a chook pen has been flooded and left to bake in the sun for a few days. I took a step forward and then stopped when the mound beneath my feet began to crumble. The sweat was running down my cheeks as I realised that whatever it was, it had been in the shed a long time. I edged along the wall to my left until my hand made contact with bales. I took a pinch of the contents and smelt it. Lucerne. Really good stuff: cured patiently and baled in the evening moisture the way my father did it. At least the farmer was feeding the animal. I became easier. It wasn't a meat eater. Perhaps it was his favourite heifer. An hysterical chuckle rose in my throat. Kids at school had often laughed about sheep farmers and their favourite stock. I relaxed. The bloody thing was being looked after. I took a step away from the wall and turned towards the door.

Before I could register the sound of slashing chain, something had ripped my shoulder. I panicked when I realised the thing was gripping on to me, like some gigantic spider I couldn't shake off. The pain became intense as the claw fastened its hold and gouged deeper. I knew what it was then: a fuckin' big roo.

I fell away from it at the door. The bloody thing was tethered and had waited until I came within reach. The slashing noise was the roo whacking its rope halter against the chain that attached it to the back wall. Even in the dark it knew its strength.

Outside, I realised my shoulder was something of a mess, but it wasn't bleeding profusely; the claw had given me a massive abrasion rather than multiple cuts. I took a crowbar from near the door and jemmied off one side of the rusting iron wall. I was angry. If the farmer had returned then he would have got a thrust of the crowbar in his head.

As a child I had hunted roos, when I'd been taken on clearing hunts. Faster through the thick lignum than adults, and careless of wild pig, I ran closer to the dogs. Once I had witnessed an extraordinary event. A roo baled up by dogs beside a low summer river took a cool look at his position as more stag hounds appeared on the bank. Ignoring for the moment a dog worrying at his hip, with two bounds he was into the river. The magnificent creature turned then and calmly drowned the first dog to reach him, a stag hound with a strain of bull terrier noticeable in its wider skull. The roo bent awkwardly with his short arms, exposing his neck, but he caught the dog and pushed it beneath the surface, holding it there while another swam around him. Suddenly he looked up the bank at me. It was the most uncanny moment: not only was he coping with the two dogs, he was also wondering how to deal with me in a strategic sense. But he was exhausted. While the first dog was already floating away, the roo stretched one arm sideways to grasp the second dog and his left arm stuck out high to one side where it bounced with his heart beats.

'Shoot the bastard!' an adult hunter screamed at me, misguidedly assuming that I was upset by the sight. I turned my rifle towards my fellow hunter; but in the same moment he blew open the roo's chest with a cut down Lee Enfield

303. He turned and winked at me, obviously exhilarated by the situation. 'Nailed the cunt,' he said. I didn't know at the time what I had been about to do; my motive had been removed from the scene by a speeding bullet.

The roo in the shed was big. His size told me he wasn't a local variety. Greys didn't have such massive shoulder development. He was tethered by his neck like a dog and must have learned not to get tangled in the rope. I shut the door of the shed so that if I could manage to release him, I'd be able to make it to a tall tree before he worked his way out through the framework of the wall.

Very little blood was running from my shoulder and it wasn't hampering my efforts. I pulled a sheet of corrugated iron from the back wall where the roo was tethered to a heavy iron ring. I undid the chain and, playing him like one of dad's yearling colts in a yard, I got him off balance with a pull from the side and brought him down, drawing the rope several times around a shed support. Round posts can slip rope easily, while still holding it firm and tight when the slightest pressure is applied from the holding end. But having him like that was useless because I couldn't undo the dog collar without him reaching me with his claws. He thumped a few times with his mighty hind legs, bringing them well up on his neck and sweeping them down as if in warning. The poor bastard was outraged. I tied him down with his neck close to a shed support and went looking for beer bottles. If this was the sort of place I understood it to be, there would be evidence. I'd never heard of roo-baiting, but I'd seen dogfights after pig-hunts, and I knew of cockfighting. They'd simply tie this old man roo to a tree and set the dogs on him, betting on how many he could kill or maim before he went down. There'd be something of a bullfight about it, but with the Australian flavour of making do with your materials. The action would be fantastic; movements that the men could incorporate in their own fight for survival. They were, most of them, only a decade out of the war and wouldn't have forgotten any of the lessons about surviving in the midst of insanity. These bloody old bush soldiers still needed violence and excitement and boozing to recall their times of glory.

The bottles had been tossed from the clearing into the edge of the scrub. I broke one against another and came back to the roo. His growls ended in hisses which couldn't simply mean that he was short of wind. I sliced through the knot in the collar that had been tied, rather than a new buckle hole punched. When the leather split, I flung the bottle on the ground and ran for a tree where I watched him from about three metres up. He walked along inside the framework of the shed, his forearms and massive tail supporting the forward movement of the hind legs, and then as quick as a mouse he was through. He stood high for a moment and I began to be uneasy, but he moved off through the scrub in a low hopping motion without checking on me.

I climbed down and left the clearing along the grey sand track. I tried to jog but the throbbing in my shoulder slowed me down to a walk.

I was glad the evening was warm. Once when I was flung from a horse I'd had to walk home through cold winds while my bruises hardened, and I kept thinking how easily I could die. My morale didn't improve until I realised that the only reason I felt so bad was that the fall had been my own fault, and that it would be ridiculous to die from such petty pride.

Except for the pain in my shoulder, I felt mildly elated, and it seemed only minutes before I was back at the guest house. I'd had one more experience of how finely balanced a human being is: if I had been chased by the animal and hadn't been able to display dominance, I would now be a quivering wreck.

The mob was already at dinner. I went through to my room, stripped off my shirt and shorts, left my door open to show my parents I was back, and walked into the bathroom. The wound on my shoulder wasn't so bad now that I could see it. I had imagined a gaping excision of flesh, although the three gashes still looked deep. I showered, dousing my shoulder with diluted Dettol. After I'd dried myself with rather affected delicacy and some unnecessary puffing, I went to the dining-room. My parents saw instantly that something was wrong. Dad was practical and secretive.

'You'll have to go to the doctor. Do you feel like a meal first?' His voice was a concerned whisper.

'Yes, I'll eat,' I said.

He looked at me studiously. 'Have you told me everything?' I nodded.

'The police will have to be told,' he said.

'Sure,' I said.

'Are you certain?' The suggestion had been some sort of test.

'Yes,' I said.

'We'd better think this through,' he said.

'Talk to the judge,' my mother said.

'Yes. We don't really know anybody here,' he added.

'This is important,' my mother said. I watched her face as she spoke, and I saw that the two of them had shared secrets before. She was flicking through the suggestions as she tested them with her experience of secrets. Life on bush farms depended, they thought, on keeping very still mouths — even when neighbours' wives disappeared, stock went missing in great quantities, and mysterious fires broke out when the wind was right.

My meal arrived promptly, set down by a smiling waitress in a black dress with a neat white apron and collar. She was on university vacation. Gillian might be up here next year I thought. The Kings for schoolgirls, and the guest house for university students.

'The doctor will be alright?' my mother queried.

'What does he tell him?' my father rejoined. 'That he was attacked by a kangaroo?'

'He was,' she said.

'But it's bloody rare stuff.'

'I could say I bailed it up, that it was a sick one.'

'Does it have to be a kangaroo?' my mother asked.

'It does,' I said. 'The claw marks are distinctive.'

'Come on,' she said, 'I'll have a look at it.' Without a thought that I might not follow, and no concern for my uneaten meal, she left the table.

On the verandah she stopped to look at the wound. I unbuttoned my shirt and lowered my shoulder. The light was bright and thousands of summer insects were smashing themselves against the wire.

'I haven't seen anything like it,' she said. 'I'll have to take it up to the hospital.' The town had a bush nursing hospital with a doctor who turned up several times a week in restricted dispensary hours.

'Just running up to see the nurse,' she reported to my father who wandered out as we were leaving. 'It's quite nasty.'

Once out of the drive my mother voiced her suspicions. 'It looks as if it could be a bite mark,' she said. I laughed. It was always my mother's way to ask the questions that broke new ground, or that provided my old man's ammunition.

'You mean a bite given at the height of passion?' I jibed. If that was what they looked like, sex was not going to be one of my most popular activities. I had read of love bites, but only in the way a callow adolescent keeps such images as fuel for fantasies.

'I'm not sure what I mean,' my mother said.

'But it's behind my shoulder . . . almost,' I said. That didn't seem to give her much reassurance. She changed gears on the old V8 with a savage thrust.

I like the aura most nurses have about them: their straightforward manner, and the way their competence and uniform somehow make them attractive, even if they are not naturally that way. Our school nurse had been terrific for a while but I think loneliness eventually wore her down. And nurses in small hospitals have a similar position of power in relation to a local community: the power to do something constructive, or not, as the case may be. My mother liked this one immediately.

'Well what have we got here?' she said.

'I seem to have got clawed,' I pronounced.

'You certainly have.' Her hands on my shoulder were gentle. They stroked around the wound, pressing a bit here and there. Then she walked around in front of me, took a basin from a cupboard, filled it, and reached for a disinfectant. But when she asked what sort of animal it was, she turned to face me with all the preparations still in her hands. Her eyes were very clear and level and I saw that she would only believe the truth.

'A kangaroo,' I said. 'It had a go at me.'

'And what were you doing to it?'

'Letting it go,' I said. 'It was tied up.'

'Whereabouts?' she asked as she motioned for my mother to hold a towel under the wound.

'Up the back of the town. It was in a shed there.'

'Whose shed?' she began probing the wound with a swab.

'Shit,' I said catching my breath quickly.

'It'll hurt a bit,' she informed me, 'but its all part of making it better.' She was one of the old school: purify everything with pain.

'No idea,' I said. 'It's in the bush country.'

'Well . . . Now there are a few straggly bits here I'll

have to snip off. They aren't going to help at all. You won't feel it. Just don't move!' And she slipped a needle with a tetanus shot into the fleshy part of my arm, then dressed the wound, finishing with a bandage that ran around my chest several times to accommodate the awkward position of the injury.

'Now that will have to be dressed every day, although I think it'll heal quite quickly.' She stood back to examine the effect.

'Wait here for a moment,' she said, 'I'd like a quick word with your mother.'

Treated like a child at boarding school for the past six years, I could have let her get away with it. Instead I insisted with a smile: 'I'm the walking wounded. I should hear it all.' Speculative silence followed my gentle challenge to the conspiracy of adults.

The dispensary was small and very white. The three of us were suspended in the heat still contained there from the afternoon. Out the window was a church, and beyond that, over the highway, a camping ground. It was quite full. Kerosine lamps burned behind the canvas. There were also several caravans looking like distorted eggs in the light from the toilet block.

'About the kangaroo,' the nurse said, 'I wouldn't mention it to anyone. There are some people around here who are a really bad lot.'

'Does that include the police?' I asked.

'I'd think twice about it.' She was leaning back against the dispensary table, arms folded. Her forearms were brown and shiny with the freshness of moisture, and the fundamental colours of a dark rainbow glistened on her skin.

'It must be pretty bad around here then,' I said. 'For the locals I mean.'

'The person I think might be responsible is a very bad lot,' she replied.

I pulled on my shirt and buttoned it. The nurse threw out the remains of the dressings.

'We'll follow your advice,' my mother said. At the door I caught the significant glance between the nurse and my mother.

In the car, as we rattled over the bridge, I asked my mother what she thought about mentioning it to the judge.

'Your father will already have done that.'

'Do you think he could do anything?'

'He is on holidays,' she said. 'And anyway, I don't think your father would like you to get mixed up with it.'

'You mean he'd like me to learn how everything works, and then shut up . . . ?'

'I didn't say that.'

'You don't have to treat me like a bloody child.'

'We always will,' she said. 'That's the way of parents.'

'Bullshit,' I said, trying for instant means to prove my manhood and independence.

'I should at least see the cop they have here,' I said, and then added, 'That's the least I could do.'

'Sister Gibbons was against you going to the police. She thought it would do no good.'

It was the attitude I had grown up with. We always thought we were getting away with things if we didn't raise our heads. The deep pools should go on reflecting the ordinary.

'Why did you send me away to school?' I asked her as were passing the Kings. I looked for Gillian's garage but the lights weren't on and its shape had disappeared into the high hedge behind.

'It was the best thing for you. You'll have those boys for friends the rest of your life.' I laughed at that. I had always been sure I would never speak to those school kids again. Not if I saw them first.

'Is that all?' I sighed. 'For friends . . .'

44

'And a good education,' she said as she spun the heavy wheel to take the gravelled track into the guest house. God, I thought, parents are ignorant. I wondered how they would have reacted if they'd seen their children being run naked around the oval and whipped with willow branches, for being too fresh to their seniors. It made me laugh to think my parents had always assumed that I was safely tucked away at school. For the last six years I had been battling to survive. The bullying at school was not something I mentioned to my parents. They didn't seem to have the capacity to understand or believe the extremes of behaviour. They'd already rationalised their own experiences.

We walked up the stairs to the verandah. Behind us the summer town was dotted with lights. I decided that my parents would not understand the hatred I carried in my guts for that farmer. For them, he was simply an extension of 'fuckin' school bullies, mate'. It was going to be something of a pleasure to subject him to the lawless state of mind of an institutionalised vandal. But then wasn't he precisely one of that species also?

At the top of the stairs my mother said, 'You'll have to rest. The shock hasn't hit you yet.' She touched me on the back. I looked at her and caught her surprise. It was years since she had touched me, and the hardness of my back was a shock to her.

'I'm alright,' I said. 'I've been hurt worse than this.' She didn't believe me. But it was my internal wounds that were still raw.

'Alright?' my father asked my mother as we entered the room.

'Yes, it'll be alright. But he needs rest.'

'What's it all about? What have you got yourself into?'

He had his hands in the pockets of his shorts and he sat down and crossed his legs. Then instead of carrying on with this challenging demeanour, he leaned across to get a book and began flicking through it. Easy movements. He used this technique while he moved closer to an animal or human. To look an animal in the eyes is confrontation. You frighten animals if you conduct yourself with unusual purpose. If you strolled, or worked on a fence while you closed with them, you could turn easily and slaughter them once you were in range. My father hated to eat meat from an animal that had been stirred up the moment it was killed. It was always too tough as far as he was concerned.

Right now my father was trying for range. If he could close on my story and understand my response he was halfway to beating me.

'It's nothing,' I said as casually as possible. 'It's just some bastard has an animal-baiting entertainment in the bush up the back there, and it seems the locals all go along with it.'

That stopped him for a moment. But as a manoeuvre, he appealed to my logic: 'I know,' he said disarmingly, 'that you're pretty sensitive to the things that are going on. I mean your teachers say that you're bright, amazingly bright, and that this can lead, well . . . to over-reaction.'

'Yeah, I don't like filling my head with shit; that's right anyway.'

'We're talking about here, right?' he demanded.

'Sure,' I said.

'What do you think should be done about it?'

'Nothing.'

'You'd better not. It's to be left to the authorities.'

'What authorities?'

'The police here.'

'The police are not to be informed. Right mum?'

My father gave her a tight glance. The book lay forgotten in his hands. She shrugged. He closed the book with a snap, pursed his lips in thought, and then said, 'Well, we'll think of something. I'll talk to Ralph.'

'That would be good,' I said.

'These things can't be let go. But there are a variety of ways they can be treated.'

'Fine,' I said. 'I'll go to bed then. I feel a bit tired.'

The night was cool. In the bedroom I put on a jumper and dropped out the window to the flower bed. I had no idea of the time, but I wanted to go out again without telling my parents who would just earbash me with tedious arguments against it.

At the Kings I asked for Gillian, but was told she had gone to bed.


CHAPTER 3

It was already hot early next morning when the pain in my shoulder woke me. Mum dressed the wound before breakfast, then I stood next to the shower and splashed myself. I felt much easier than I'd expected to. It was as if I had earned a rest. I could hang around the guest house without feeling guilty, or being made to feel that I should be exerting myself on the beach because of my youth. I had earned a place among the adults. But if I was around to talk to they earbashed me about how much work they'd done, or how they were quiet heroes, and knew all the stuff. It could make you ill if you listened to too much of it. But this morning I was my own hero.

The lawn was still damp after breakfast and gleamed with secret portions of sunlight. For about fifteen minutes each morning, there was a strip of sun that extended the length of the two north hedges. I walked through them and down to the tennis courts. Hans and the judge were lobbing away at each other. I liked watching the game, but hated playing it. For some reason I disliked revealing a competitive nature in public. Rachel was on a garden seat with a book, ignoring the sweaty effort going into the game. I sat to watch. The grass wasn't too damp so I leaned back on my hands and crossed my legs in front of me. Rachel closed her book.

'How are you this morning?' she asked.

'Alright I think,' I said smiling and raised a hand to touch my shoulder in a gesture of embarrassment.

'It was something funny?' she asked. 'Some funny business, yes?'

'Not too funny,' I said, determined never again to produce a wet adolescent smile whenever somebody spoke to me.

'It was a kangaroo. Somebody baits them with dogs. I think they make bets on what happens. That sort of thing anyway.'

'Yes,' she said casually. 'People are pigs.' Ridiculously, I had expected her to be genteelly shocked. I had accepted her appearance without considering her courageous survival. Such brutality, for her, was only to be expected.

'Aaaaah,' I began with a stutter. 'Do they ever stop?'

'I do not think so,' she said leaning with one arm over the back of the seat, dropping the book beside her. 'I think they will always be the same. You stopped this?'

'No, I just let it go.'

'What will happen to the people who do this?'

'Nothing. Nobody is too worried.' Right at this moment I didn't give a stuff either.

'People should be worried by such behaviour. If laws are not used, people don't think much of them.' Her eyes were sharp. She knew where my responsibility lay.

'The locals here aren't too worried. They probably think it's just like the shooting they do with live birds. They trap galahs for that, or breed pigeons.'

'Yes,' she said. 'People like killing; they like it like playing God.'

I chewed the inside of my lips and nodded, looking down at the grass. She laughed, and I thought it was at me, but she was looking at the game. She looked across at me.

'Men say they have to kill to stop the killing, but really they like doing it. They think it might be exciting, and then they like it. Sometimes later they have bad dreams. But I have no pity for them. It only takes a little bit of thought.'

I had nothing to say. An experienced woman, who had survived hell and studied the inmates, had just delivered a completely authoritative summation. There was no room for discussion. Preoccupied, she raised her hand with the tip of her thumb almost touching her finger tip. 'That much thought,' she added.

'They're really country boys,' I said. 'I think that's the reason. We've all seen how animals can be treated, you know.'

'I have been one of those animals. And it's not only farm boys. The others catch up very quickly.'

'I'm sorry,' I muttered. 'I realise I don't know these things, but I can understand you.'

'Nobody understands anything, finally,' she said. 'Most people think they have all the right attitudes and are satisfied with that. So when something different begins they have no other reference points to discover where they are, and they make all the old mistakes. Things are never the same. You might guard against the worst thing you know, but the new thing will grow slowly — a slow horror — and all the old attitudes won't be able to cover it. Nobody is ever ready.'

I watched the two men playing on the court. The judge was light on his feet, but Hans, unskilled as he was, could hit a ball hard. It was a beautiful morning. The clear sky, the fresh green lawn and the sound of surf rising above the bank of dunes were exhilarating. I was absorbing a lesson, an extraordinary one, and yet I could only regard it as mulch for my brain. As an unrelated idea, it gave me no base for action. But then perhaps very few people could cope with it. I certainly had no way of placing it in the jigsaw of my mind and anyone I told would be predisposed to disbelief.

I looked across at her. In a light blue linen dress, her legs crossed, one foot swinging slightly, her handsome profile was silhouetted against the sky over the dunes. How lucky she was, I thought, to be here, on this marvellous morning a decade after the horror.

'You mean people never reflect enough to grow?' I asked.

'We think enough,' she said. 'We just don't take any responsibility for it.'

The ball on the court flew back and forth, belted by imitation athletes. Rachel pushed back her hair.

'This thing that is going on here, this is not unusual. You must understand that. Animals are practised on. They have no idea what is happening. It is not so different herding animals, from herding people.'

'I'm sorry,' I said, feeling totally abject and apologizing more for my lack of an adequate response.

'Hans,' she called to her husband, 'you are carrying too much weight.' He smiled at her gratefully. She looked down at me.

'You must not think too much about what I say. It is nothing.'

'No,' I said. 'I think I understand.'

'You must look after that shoulder,' and again she held up her thumb and forefinger almost touching. 'There is only that much difference between getting well and getting sick.'

I watched Hans and the judge struggle for a bit longer, then still preoccupied, I walked up to the entrance of the guest house. Leaning on the verandah, I looked across at the bald dunes above the ti-tree line. The sound of the waves was whip-like, and I imagined the water slashing down in a dumping pattern. I knew about the things Rachel had been saying; I knew that I had often been tempted not to analyse my experiences. And she'd made me conscious of the fact that I had accepted violence as a valid method of solving problems: a matter of getting in first.

I walked across the road into the dunes and lay on a slope watching the ocean move, dazzled by the blue. I understood then that most people reached the limit of their inner resources all too quickly, so that violence became a solution arrived at out of habit, or for want of imagination.

At the Kings the juke box was thumping out the new music from America: rock and roll, while the kids washed down the cement floor. It had been painted red last year and already it looked like the floor of a toilet block. But although the cement needed another coat of paint, the bright displays and the cleanliness of the place made it welcoming. Gillian came through the swinging doors from the kitchen balancing metal milkshake containers. She deposited them in rows, then walked up to the greengrocer's section where she started to build a stack of oranges.

'Hey,' I said, 'you've known all along about that mad farmer bastard?' She stopped and rested her hands on the fruit stand.

'What do you mean?'

'The bloodhouse he's got up the back. Where he kills the animals.'

'Haven't a clue,' she said.

'What do you mean then? You've been frightened as hell of him.'

'What do *you* mean?'

'I followed him last night after I left you. He had an old roo tied up in a shed. The whole place looked bad. You know, there were signs around that he had killed animals up there.'

'You mean he does his own butchering?'

'Come on,' I said, 'roo meat?'

'My parents lived on roo meat during the depression. They liked it.' She began assembling the oranges.

'No, this had the feel of an illicit place. You know a blood dump when you see one. You run across them in the bush sometimes. Clearings where a lot of people have been involved in a lot of activity: gambling on animals or birds. I came across a place once where hundreds of galahs had been shot by sportsmen. It was like hundreds of pillows had been split. Feathers all over the bushes like snow... This place out the back had ropes hung in trees. I'd say they tie the roos and set the dogs on them.'

'God,' Gillian exclaimed, and threw an orange at the back of the stand. 'That's foul, disgusting. There aren't people like...' she trailed away. 'What would they bet on?'

'How many dogs it slit, or killed. How long it lasted. Anything.'

Gillian rubbed the ball of her palm several times along the side of the stand. 'What can we do?'

'I let the roo go last night. They obviously trucked it in from the north. It was a big red.'

She shivered slightly as if something clammy had touched her. 'I don't feel like getting mixed up in anything.'

'Who said you would be?'

'You are aren't you?' She turned away from the vegetable stand, tossing an orange from hand to hand. Her look was challenging.

'Don't know. But I want to know what you know.'

'It's nothing like that,' she sighed.

If I burst out with all the questions I wanted to ask I'd look pretty uncool. 'I'll see you later anyway. I'm just holding you up here.'

I looked at her, and was again filled with frustration at all my unexpressed affection. 'See you then,' I said, and she grinned back.

As I opened the door she called: 'You've got blood on your shirt!'

'I was wounded last night,' I laughed.

'What?' she said

'I'll swap stories with you later.'

The day's convalescence enabled me to watch the guest house. My father's car was parked under a small tree on a slope that gave me a view over most of the recreation area. Settled in the back seat with a novel, I had the house out the rear window, out the side window the small bungalows beyond the hedge, and the tennis court out the front window. The heat hadn't reached the car in the shadow of the tree, so with the windows open I would be comfortable until lunchtime.

At about ten o'clock the waitresses had a break from their work and came down to play tennis. A few minutes later Arthur Waterhouse emerged from the guest house with a golf stick and began putting a golf ball around the lawn. Soon he was nudging the ball back and forth beside the tennis court. Arthur looked really sharp in his peaked American cap and Bermuda shorts, and he carried on some desultory conversation with the girls. It was inhibited of course by their playing and his playing, but it seemed he was offering them his services. They regarded his suggestions with something akin to hilarity. From the snatches of conversation that reached me I gathered he was helping the girls discuss their futures. I understood Arthur's intentions absolutely; they didn't have a great deal to do with the insurance company he worked for, although he did mention its policy of hiring young students for the legal department. His voice took on a kind of American accent as he talked. I didn't know he'd been to America, although I did remember he'd talked of something called 'motels' that would beat the hell out of guest house living.

At ten thirty a small group descended from the verandah for a morning walk along the cliffs. Accompanying my parents were the judge, his wife, and Mrs Waterhouse. None of the group looked down towards Arthur who waved his golf stick in a vague salute. The men were in shorts and the women in flowery dresses. My father sported a shapeless white hat, green under the brim, and zinc cream on his nose. The judge was similarly attired except that his shorts stuck out from his legs the way a child might draw them on a stick figure. Sarah had a straw hat with a brim so huge that even in the slightest breeze it would flop back and she'd look like a cowgirl galloping across the range. Before they walked out the gate under the arch of the hedge, Arthur called out to watch for cliff falls. They all laughed heartily. The girls on the court played their shots with enthusiasm.

The only other person I saw that morning was the young law graduate, Anthony Falkiner, who had been given a red pre-war racing Jaguar as a present. He was a chubby sort of bugger who had a good sense of humour — or so he imagined, because he laughed a great deal — and a manner that made all the oldies respect him. He and his car had created quite a sensation amongst the staff when he first drove up and there was considerable speculation about him. He was immediately regaled by the judge with stories about the law course at Melbourne University — he had completed his course at Sydney University. However, he didn't flirt with them and his red car remained undriven, under a tarpaulin at the back of the guest house. When I asked him why he didn't drive it, he told me there was no point, that it was expensive because it only did seven miles to the gallon. He was one of those complacent individuals who derive enough satisfaction from sitting back and gloating over the things they possess. Very rarely do one of his kind look up and notice, or even care, that the world has passed them by. The judge said Anthony was very well connected. I remembered my mother saying to my father once, that out of twelve judges on the Supreme Court in Victoria, eleven of them had been educated at Scotch College. So Anthony was well on his way.

I saw Anthony walk past the clothes-line next to the bungalows, stop for a moment to look at the finery hanging there, and then disappear down between the hedges to the entrance of the tennis courts. He obviously thought he had the grounds to himself because he stepped onto the court without racquet or opponent and began to serve and return with consummate skill. It was a delight to watch. After each imaginary game, he would leap over the net like a gazelle. I thought, well, it's not that different from body-surfing or any of your other loner sports.

Anthony left the court in a proper sweat, having come very close to being thrashed by his 'opponent'. That spectacle over, I became absorbed in my novel and had no idea of how much time had passed when I looked up again. Some rugs were being shaken outside one of the side doors and the sound of a saw came from Les's workshop at the back of the house. I got out of the car and stretched until a spasm of heat-pain shot through my shoulder. I tossed the novel into the back seat and walked around the side of the building past the bungalows to speak to Les.

As I rounded the corner Arthur was backing out the door of one of the staff bungalows. When he turned I tried to look embarrassed that I had caught him out. He avoided my stare, so I guessed he was feeling uncomfortable.

Les was constantly involved in planning or conducting renovations on the old guest house. I think its genteel and shabby elegance troubled him. He would have preferred something with lines that had a respectable geometry, perhaps brick and not weatherboard. The large black-tiled bathrooms, new this summer, were outrageous. My mother said they were in appalling taste: like having black satin sheets on the beds. I thought they were terrific and managed an erection most times I was showering mid-afternoon while guests were on the beach. I thought Les must have built them so he could have fun chasing his pale wife around in them during the off-season.

The workshop stood in the shade of some big gums with low branches.

'Good place to work,' I said. He nodded absently as he checked measurements. It was a great work room in that nothing was out of place and it looked fully equipped. There was an immense amount of wood stacked neatly at one end.

'Building more bungalows?' I asked. He looked up as though he was only beginning to understand that someone was talking to him. I admired the absolute concentration of many expert workmen, how they spend hours in a trance-like state and accomplish phenomenal amounts of work. I'd seen my father in the same state. But it was misleading, because once the love of crafting is put under pressure, the craft becomes work again. And if craftsmen take on more work than they can handle the workroom becomes a place of torture.

'No,' he said. 'Just some renovations.' He had the right idea: it removed him from the routine of scrubbing, cleaning and cooking, while still — and rightly — convincing people like his wife that he was putting in maximum effort. (But I bet his wife didn't do her work in a transcendental state.)

He lifted a piece of timber onto the bench and sighted along it, stroked it, and then marked it.

'Do you know the old farmer that keeps the shed up the back?' I asked.

Les stopped working and put the knuckles of both hands on the workbench.

'I heard about last night. Just keep away from the mad bastard. He's dangerous.' He gave me a speculative look. 'I mean that.'

'I was just wondering.'

Les picked up a plane. He had felt in the wood an unevenness that was impossible to see.

'Fuckin' dangerous to do too much wondering,' he said. 'Larra came back from the war like that. It turned a lot of them into mad bastards.'

'A lot like him around here?' I asked.

'There's a few.' He paused. 'Mainly they talk a lot and get on the piss, but they keep some bad habits.'

'What do they say about him around here?'

'They reckon he's only half there, but they don't mind him.'

'What about the stuff that happens up the shed?'

'They don't want to know about it.'

I walked back to the car to retrieve my novel. It was *The Young Lions*, by Irwin Shaw, and had been donated to the school library, then banned from it. As secretary of the Debating Society and a mate of the bloke on the Library Committee, I had scored it. I was engrossed in this novel because it seemed to give some explanation of war, of the clues needed to survive it. Other war novels I'd read were written by observers, or people who wanted to be associated with heroism; unlike *The Young Lions*, they didn't reveal the violence of war to be in essence shabby dogshit.

The car was hot now and I lay down beside it to continue

reading. But the roar of the surf had heightened with the incoming tide, and guests were crunching past on the gravel, wending their way to lunch.

Rachel and Hans walked up the stairs in front of me. Her legs were long and tanned. Life since her persecution had filled them out to the required shape, but there was something infirm about the flesh. It shook slightly, as if it had no muscle support. As Hans went forward to open the door, I saw deep scars above Rachel's knees and awful gouges in the flesh on her thighs. Before such evidence I felt hopelessly lacking in knowledge and experience.

I didn't wait for my parents before I ordered. They were probably still idling around the cliffs somewhere. I enjoyed eating on my own in the half-empty dining-room. I thought mostly about Gillian. Her friendship had become a valuable element in my sustaining some regard for myself.

In the late afternoon I walked down to the Kings to meet her. We walked along the river to the beach, trudging happily through the soft white sand to the east of the dunes. This lonely stretch of sand had built up during the high tides and pounding surf of the winter and curved from the dunes for about four hundred metres to the rocky headland and the beginning of the cliffs. It had blocked the flow of the river entirely. We stopped several times just to feel the beauty of the place. Closer to the ocean we sat listening to the lapping of the waves that shallowed as they washed over the reef a few metres below the surface.

Gillian didn't mention my wound and I didn't mention the farmer. Not until we arrived at the main beach where she wanted to swim between the lifesavers' flags.

'Did you swim today?' she asked.

'No,' I said. 'I'm recovering.'

'What do you mean?'

'My wound.'

'Your what?' she laughed.

'Don't you remember? You told me I had blood on my shirt this morning.'

'Oh!' she exclaimed. 'I thought it was a joke. Ros said it was a joke.'

'Which one is Ros?' I asked.

'My friend,' she said.

'The tall girl, the one who talks to the customers all the time?'

Gillian laughed. 'She was innoculated with a gramophone needle.'

'Anyway, it's not a joke,' I persisted. 'I'm a genuine hero!'

'Really,' she said sceptically.

'I told you about the roo. The bloody thing grabbed me.'

I told her the whole story of following the farmer, and then my own conclusions.

When I looked across at her again she had withdrawn.

'I'm going home in a few days,' she murmured after a tense silence.

'Hell no!' I said. 'It can't be that bad. Nothing is that bad. I mean if you're frightened it can be worked out. I mean I probably exaggerated it a bit.'

'You don't know about being frightened,' she said. 'You've just been playing games.'

'Alright,' I said placatingly as I leaned towards her on my elbow. 'Jesus I know that. I mean I wouldn't do anything unless I had a pretty good idea I'd get away with it. But I can fix a problem.' Remembering her response when she first saw him on the dunes I added, 'If it's the farmer you're frightened about I can bloody well do something about that.'

'Yes,' she said with a solemn face. 'It is the farmer and you can't ...' She sat up quickly. '... do anything about it. He's completely insane.' She stood up and pulled her bathers tight over her bottom. When she looked down at me, tall and willowy, her hair falling over her face, it occurred to me that she could afford to take risks. She threw her hair back and looked at the sea, then folded her arms and squirmed her feet hard into the sand.

'I'll tell you about it,' she said. 'Sometime.'

I watched her walk down to the water, where she hesitated for a moment like an elegant and uncertain horse, doubtful of the texture it was about to walk on, and then she turned and smiled at me. I became aware that people had been looking at her and now, as she walked in, they looked at me. They wanted to see the person lucky enough to receive that smile. I was cool though. In a fraction of a moment I had left behind my tendency towards embarrassment.

With the tide still high the waves were rolling well, sweeping the soup area continually — that area where the ocean churns, stirred unceasingly, and where sometimes it's hard to plough through when the big waves compress into a metre and a half of hard white water. The casual surfer can easily lose enthusiasm. But Gillian was through it in a minute, duck-diving under four massive walls of water. Beneath the waves she would have been hanging close to the sand with fingers and toes dug deep, in case the turbulence dropped below the surface. Her lack of fuss in the water made for economy of energy. Out the back she lay waiting for a big wave. She kicked her feet in the air several times. When the chosen wave arrived she caught the slope easily, sliding down the face of moving green glass. She kicked herself forward and held speed through the soup. My feeling for her at that moment was one of sheer anticipation tingling through the tissues of my shoulders and neck. It was a feeling I hadn't experienced since childhood. I hoped I could hang onto it.

The wave pushed her right to the sand and for a moment

she was helpless, her long rounded limbs tossing, almost independently. Recovered, she stood up laughing and walked back into the sea to wash the sand from her togs. She smiled up at me again and it was as if she intuited everything: not only my admiration then for her gleaming body, but all the melodrama of adolescent romance. I knew I had a lot more to learn about women, but she was extraordinary.

'It's a pity you can't come in,' she said as she walked back, squeezing the water from her hair with quick twists of her hands over one shoulder.

'It is,' I said staring past her legs at the colourful figures romping in the water. And then it came to me: *I'll burn the bastard out.* Fire was fear to a farmer. It could make them physically ill when they smelt smoke on a north wind and their skin told them it was a dry and dirty day. At home lots of fires came out of the north doing only strategic damage. Perhaps I'd only threaten him with fire. I was aware then that without her telling me a thing I'd accepted the fact of Gillian having suffered in some way, and the need for it to be righted.

I caught myself looking up at the dunes to see whether the farmer had come down to perve on the late swimmers, or watch the ocean.

'What were you looking at?' Gillian asked as I turned back.

'Our mate,' I said.

She flicked sand at me with her foot.

'It's not funny,' she said.

'I don't know that I think it is.'

'I'm sure that you wouldn't...'

'Why don't you find out?'

'It'll make you angry. I think it will anyway.' She sat down in front of me facing the dunes and leaned forward over crossed legs.

'Hey,' I said, 'this is going to be serious.' I kept stroking the sand beside me.

'I think it is,' she said. 'I'm telling you something I'd told myself I'd never think about again.'

She told me that a few weeks ago she had been out with a boy who had shown her the sights along the coast. They tooled along the Great Ocean Road in his sports car and parked in secluded places above the ocean. She and the boy had got along pretty well. He wasn't a persistent battler. After driving back to Anglecrest he had suggested a few drinks before he took her home. They drove up to the hotel where the boy knew someone, so they were guided through into the lounge. There were a couple of dozen people there including some other girls. But immediately she felt the farmer eyeing her steadily. He wouldn't stop staring, and although she had been the focus of stares before, she began to feel uncomfortable. The farmer was drinking with a few cronies, but they were well into convivial drinking and didn't notice the man's interest in her. Becoming more and more uneasy she asked the boy to take her back to the Kings.

She had been in the garage only a few minutes when Fat Thomas, the owner of the Kings, turned up and asked if she would talk to him outside. She followed him reluctantly, and they walked around to the side of the cafe. There were some men, three men, standing beside an old car, and Fatso said, this is such and such, and she hadn't remembered their names. She nodded and began to make moves to leave, saying to Fatso that she was working the early shift. He said: don't worry about it. She couldn't see his face and wondered at the lack of light; there were only the night lights on the petrol bowsers and the light over the cash register behind the window. Fatso had left then: 'I'll leave you to get friendly.' The farmer had been leaning on the car and stood away from it suddenly.

'Like to take a little ride,' the farmer said. 'Up in the hills away from everyone. We wouldn't hurt you, you know.' He took her arm and she pulled away. One of the men stepped between her and an escape path.

'Come on now,' the farmer said. 'Just sit in the car if you like, we're your friends.' The other men laughed.

She pulled away hard, jerking her arm, but couldn't free herself.

'I'll call the police,' she'd said.

'You don't have to,' the farmer said, 'they're here.'

One of the men hit the side of the car with his hand, threw back his head and said, 'Jesus Larra'. The farmer laughed at him and then turned all his attention to Gillian. 'Come on,' he said. 'I know what girls like you want. You mightn't think it but a lot of little girls around here know.' She stood petrified, dreading any movement that might trigger the man into action. It was like the nightmare of running and jumping but only standing still.

'You can't just walk away from this, you know.' One of the men backed off. Too frightened to move even her eyes, in case it was misinterpreted, she could only guess it was the policeman. The farmer pinioned one of her arms behind her back, the other was trapped tight against his body. 'Come on,' he said and ran his hand up her leg and into her shorts. Without reasoning she began to scream. It rattled the bastard. 'Go on then,' he said pushing her. 'You can piss off. I couldn't get a fat anyway.' He called after her. 'If you tell anyone, we'll be back.' Then he ran after her and kicked her buttocks.

I had made suitably sympathetic sounds at the beginning of the account, but by the end I was in a rage. 'He'll die that fucking bastard,' I growled. I had never felt anything with such certainty, and that conviction began to calm me: the decision had been reached for me.

Gillian looked at me without much emotion. 'It happened

to me,' she said. 'And I don't feel so much now.' She looked down for a moment and then said. 'Everybody dies anyway.' I wasn't sure whether she was justifying my proposed action, or saying, *well what's it matter he'll get his naturally.*

'Didn't anybody hear you scream?'

'No, I don't think they did. Fatso came out the back — he must have been watching it all — and asked what was wrong, they only wanted to meet me. He wanted to get out of it. I blubbered all night in bed. In the morning I was locked into doing nothing.'

'Does he come down to the beach to watch you?'

'No, but I'd seen him before that. Down here I mean.'

I tuned out of the conversation then. She was talking but I was away and concentrating on some images forming at the back of my mind. The heat has always made me confident. Summer is a season I could live with all the year round. You can just lie in the sand or on the grass in a state of semi-consciousness, and dream. Waking from such a state had often brought the solution to problems. It's only a matter of finding the state — the right place, temperature and the desire. I knew I could lie on a bed of nails in that state. Plans for the farmer were forming in that meditative condition.

'You know,' Gillian said tapping me on the arm, knowing I was somewhere else, 'in the bathroom the next day I looked at myself in the mirror and held up my arms like a body builder, and I wondered whether I could develop muscles. It was ridiculous.'

'Not ridiculous,' I said, overwhelmed by the pity I felt for her.

She shook her head. 'It was so hopeless, and for a while I thought it had been all my fault. I thought perhaps I didn't, hadn't, learned how to handle myself.'

I had visions of the complete destruction of the man.

'No one would miss him.' I said. 'They might reckon

they like him, but they'd feel easier if he was gone.'

Gillian laughed outright. 'Don't be ridiculous,' she said. 'You know you don't mean it.'

I had never been so certain of anything. It was as if I could give her my strength. Her utter vulnerability increased my desire for her. And with that came a sweep of lust that had the strength of anything the farmer could have. I turned away from her quickly to prevent myself handling her roughly. She might have guessed the story had fascinated me, but then she'd feel insulted. Perhaps I only hated the farmer for carrying his fantasies into reality and getting away with it. I smacked the sand with my uninjured hand to camouflage the strength of my emotions.

'I've got to go up now,' she said. 'I'm filling in for Ros for a couple of hours.' She looked at me. 'You know I haven't really asked how badly you've been hurt. But when I think about you I don't really imagine you getting hurt. I don't know why.'

After dinner I went to my room to read. I feel asleep for an hour or so and woke totally refreshed. My arm had lost its stiffness and there was only the slightest drag from the wound.

A few minutes later I walked down the passage into the main hall. I heard laughter, and glancing into the lounge I caught the swaying shadows on the wall. Somebody was attempting to sing, not too raucously. The piano wasn't being used yet, but give them another half-hour and they'd be full enough to defy the wishes of proprietor Les Stuart, who had decreed that it wouldn't be played in the evenings.

At the Kings I asked for Gillian, but was told she had gone to bed early and I wasn't to go pushing around in the garage because sleep was sacred to shiftworkers. I walked out into the night again. There was a crispness to the air but the stillness piled up perfumes of the summer. I followed the sounds and then the lights to the carnival down by the gleaming water of the river. It wasn't the public spirited dancing in the streets of the carnivals in the exotic countries I had lately been wishing I would one day visit, but rather a commercial little arrangement that used the carnival image to drag in the country bumpkins. Between the laughing clowns, the horrendous octopus mechanism and the hoopla stand, you could see the bush along the seaside, and beyond the darkly oiled river, the white patches of the bald-topped dunes rising high above the ocean. Within the confines of the carnival there was movement, and people to look at. But standing there I felt somehow removed from the scene. I was panicked at first, but then I enjoyed the sensation of existing in another time zone. It was shattered when I ran into two of the crew from the surfboat that I had rowed in last year. Their sneering was all too predictable.

'Too good for us, mate?' George asked.

'Up yours,' I said.

George had huge shoulders that threatened to fracture his thin neck each time he moved quickly. His strength was not to be underestimated however. He had reached the finals in the state swimming championships over 800 yards freestyle, and his legs were exceptionally thick. You noticed them the way you might suddenly register the size and the strength of an approaching Clydesdale draught horse.

'Are you still full of bullshit?' Jack asked. Small and nuggety, his strength was one developed from broad weight and a low centre of gravity. We'd won every surfboat race on the coast the previous summer, so it was not as if any of the crew had been weaklings — not physically that is.

'Why'd you pull out?' George asked.

I shrugged. 'When you win the state finals you've won it. Next time it's...'

'We're going to do it again this summer,' Jack said. 'Without you. We don't fuckin' need you.'

'That's terrific,' I said.

'Yeah, the new bloke's got more power.'

Jack couldn't keep still. He was moving around me like a fox terrier that's surprised a frill-necked lizard in long grass and can't quite get a clear look at it.

'You alright Jack?' I asked. 'Nothing wrong with you?'

George took a step closer to me, bent on genuine inquiry. 'Why dontcha wanna be in the bloody crew?'

'I've got other things to do. You know how it is?' He didn't. He was a club member and that entitled him to companionship and a certain standing. He could mix with all the other bullshit artists and drool over the stories of older blokes' successes with women and how they made them put lipstick on again after they had slobbered off the first lot. Last summer that story had started a surge of sexual heat in the club, and the members had begun a collection of lipsticks found on the beach to use for that purpose. George had tried to impress his appeal on the rest of the club with a well-developed thirteen year old. When an older bloke had chided him on the girl's age he'd been defensively knowledgeable.

'Well all I can say,' he'd said with an experienced drawl, 'is that for a thirteen year old she's fantastic.'

We were all in the change room when he'd said this and I replied, 'Yeah, and last year she was a fantastic twelve year old.' George grabbed me in a headlock and we both fell to the floor. I was breathless but I regained balance and stood up with him in my arms. He applied more and more pressure to my neck until I felt the bottom of his strength; then I carried him outside and rubbed his back on a piece of packing case that had been dug in to reinforce the dune on which the clubhouse had stupidly been built. The packing case split and part of the dune surged through the gap, taking the two of us with it. We landed at the feet of the club president who went off his rocker at us.

'You little pricks!' he yelled. 'Fix the bloody thing.'

'He started it,' I said. 'He can do it.' I walked off.

Everybody turned a hand to fixing it and most of them wanted me kicked out of the club. I couldn't have cared less. But they decided that the run of wins the junior boat crew had been scoring couldn't be interrupted, so they had grudgingly endured me. That was possibly why I hadn't returned to the club this summer. But my reasoning still stood up pretty well: I didn't want to repeat things all my life.

Now we leaned against the side of a fairy-floss stall. There was no urge to violence. It was all just being taken as a normal abuse session. We had rowed together for so long last year that there was nothing we didn't know about each other's territories. But what I'd done — run out on the club — was disloyal and beyond their imagination.

'Most of the blokes reckon you're a poofter,' Jack said, changing the line of abuse.

'Is that right?' I said. 'Don't they know it's a proven fact that blokes who join clubs to be one of the boys are the most likely ones to turn poofter.'

'Bullshit,' George said.

'It's a known fact,' I said manufacturing my own statistics the way everybody else did. 'One out of every ten blokes is a poofter, but in clubs it's five out of ten, although most of them don't know it.'

'Well they're not poofters then,' George argued reasonably.

'You can tell 'em,' I said. 'They're always running women down.'

'Everybody I know reckons women are terrific,' George said.

'You might not be a poofter then,' I said. 'But it could come on you late in life. You don't want to let your guard down.'

'You're full of shit,' Jack said meanly.

'Do you like women?' I countered him.

'Yeah, I do,'

'Got any good stories about your life with women?' I asked him. His lip curled. Looking at him I realised that those times he'd jumped from a broaching surfboat with the rest of us and had been slow to surface, he'd been no doubt scouring the ocean floor for stray flounders to fuck.

'Sure I have,' he said, eyes darting around. 'I've done it.'

'Like hell you have, and you'll never do it!' I said.

He turned to George. 'What about the sheila you and me...'

'Need help do you? Need George's help?'

'No one needs any help,' George said pushing me in the chest with his finger, ready to job me. I grabbed his finger and bent it back. It was all ju-jitsu then, all finger holds, and George went down on one knee.

'You prick,' he said.

'Listen dick features,' I said. 'I don't want to talk to you again, ever. Do you understand that?' He refused to answer, which meant that the second I let him go he'd fly at me. I jerked his finger back and it made a noise like a frail walnut shell cracking.

'You bastard!' he screamed. 'You've broken my finger!'

He stared at his finger and then at me in disbelief. I walked away. A piece of rock flew past my head. I heard it and looked up, and as I caught a glimpse of it, the rock seemed to be travelling in a kind of slow motion. Again that weird removal. I turned back to him, but it had been Jack and Jack wasn't going to throw any more rocks.

'We'll bloody get you for this you bastard,' he shouted. He thought a threat like this would be the end of the matter.

I had had the knuckle of my small finger dislocated once by two older kids at school. They'd done it slowly, wanting me to cry for mercy. I had simply removed my mind from the pain in my finger and told myself, *OK they're going to break my finger, so what?* And the pain had become remote and controllable, and then the knuckle had popped.

I walked over to Jack and began kicking him. I knew my bandage would be too restricting for any other movement. I danced around him, kicking his shins, his arse, whatever part of his body was turned towards me. I kicked him with the tops of my toes, the way you kick a football, so there was no real pain inflicted. He didn't even try to reach me. When I pushed him on the ground he just lay there saying *Jesus, Jesus, Jesus.*

For a moment, as I walked away from the carnival, I felt exhilaration, and then I realised how stupid it all was, and especially how stupid I'd been, and I felt sick at my childishness.

In bed that night I dreamed that I had tied Gillian up in a shed and the excitement was beyond anything I had ever known. Then suddenly I became gentle with her, untying her, happy to let her go, and the excitement was the same.

## CHAPTER 4

The fires in the north of the state began to dominate the conversations around the guest house. The scorching days were not only driving everyone into the surf, they were also threatening reminders of how easily bush towns could be devastated. The papers had pages of photographs of the destruction: burnt animals, their legs grotesquely resembling stalk-detonators, piled high in the corners of blackened paddocks, swollen like marine mines; and people with charred and bandaged faces being stretchered into ambulances or doorways of bush nursing hospitals. With a shock many of the guests were reminded of the unstoppable fires that had roared through the Otways in the thirties with such devastation. Few people seemed to understand that technology would be required to control such a holocaust. Their knowledge of the elements was pitiful.

The judge thought the fires would attract rain. 'It stands to reason,' he said. 'Rain always comes after intense heat.' Personally I agreed with him, but wondered just how long after. The Squadron Leader said an enemy could conquer Australia by fire-bombing strategically when the fierce northerlies were blowing. It seemed to me that he relished such a prospect.

'I suppose you saw great fires during the war?' I asked him.

'Yes, my word. From the air they're a beautiful sight.' He humphed with an effort that travelled from his throat to his stomach. The photographs had awakened old memories, or his imagination. '*We* were always close to death too you know,' he said.

That same morning over coffee, I heard Rachel say that she smelt smoke, and others walked out onto the verandah to look for signs. Hans later told my father she often smelt smoke. It was as if her physical senses could remember the chimneys of the camps. Everybody said the fires were too far away to threaten the beaches. 'They're well over a hundred miles away,' the judge informed us all.

That evening the sunset had a raging colour. Its fierce gold filled the ocean and it seemed to descend into a steamy sea. Gillian and I walked down along the beach and through the lapping gold. The cliffs to the west displayed bright red faces. This spectacular vision gave me a feeling of the immensity of life and that I was lucky to be around for a while. My life seemed so much richer. My days were filled with Gillian. I had been the cynic, the cynic who had never made love or been in love, but had always known what girls were to be used for. I had even ridiculed blokes for their romantic attachments. They would carry around photographs of girls and whip them out and stare at them, and it had made me furiously jealous. I'd bait them about being in love: *do you really looof her*? I'd ask, making the word sound as ridiculous as possible. And now I walked around with her always somehow present: the way she walked and talked and smiled, or furrowed her broad, shapely brow. And then when I went to meet her I'd realise that the images I had been carrying with me were merely pale reflections. Several times as I walked beside her to the beach I knew that if I had spoken, my voice would have betrayed the desire I was filled with when I looked at her thighs, or in fact any part of her — I was infatuated by her whole being. So I pretended I was preoccupied, or giving her question a great deal of thought. I understood what the farmer was about, the bastard.

'I'm really glad you don't try and muck around,' she said once.

'Why?'

'Well most boys would.'

'Hey, baby,' I said hamming up dialogue from the shit films the Yanks were flooding the country with. 'I'm cool, I can live with that.'

'You're hopeless,' she laughed. Yes, I thought, I could be, but no bastard is going to know it. I'd never been the clown before though, and it felt pretty good. I leant down and gave her an affectionate hug around the hips, my grip the same as if I was going to lift her into the air. The subtle movements of her body as she continued to walk astounded me. She laughed, but a hand on my shoulder signalled me away. I bounced around her in the shallows like a puppy, and felt like barking. I was wet through when I had finished my act so I walked further out and dived under a wave.

The night sea was warm and teeming with sensations that were absent during the day. When I stood up the north wind struck me with a heat that moved through my flesh to the bones. Gillian strode out too and dived through the surface of gold. The slap of her body hung in the air where she had disappeared. This is impossible, I thought, I've never even imagined the ocean this way. I wondered if I would ever lose the memory of it. She stood up dripping and laughing. 'God, it's superb,' she gasped. She wasn't within my reach, so I splashed her with a flick of my hand on the gleaming surface, just to touch her in some way. The light left the sea. It was uncanny.

'Look,' Gillian said, and pointed to the faint glow that tinged the sky to the north. 'That must be the fires. Or are they reflected lights from the city?'

I didn't know; but it occurred to me that if you could see the effect of a catastrophe it must have some influence on the way you lived. Would it be the same if you foresaw the possibility of a catastrophe? Again, I didn't know. But that faint glow had a profound effect on me. It was the way I imagined the sound of distant guns.

'That must be how the world will begin to end,' I said.

'Shut up,' she said. 'I can't stand people who depress me.'

'Is that a warning or something?'

'No, but it's stupid.'

'I'd like to see the fires.'

'I wouldn't, I just like their effects. I don't have to see them.'

'You mean you don't like experiencing danger, just the look of it?'

'Probably.'

'I'd like to be there.'

'No imagination,' she said.

'I like to know how things really happen. I'd always like to know that.'

'That always comes to you. My aunt says everything always happens to everybody, but most people don't realise what's happening to them.'

I doubted that, but I had no arguments.

It was only about twenty minutes before our clothes dried on us — parched by the wind as we walked.

'The papers said the state is like a tinder box, that there's no moisture in anything.' An edge of anxiety modulated Gillian's voice.

'Imagine the atom bomb,' I said, thinking of the Squadron Leader's imagination.

'I couldn't do that.'

As we came to the point where the ti-tree ran from the top of the cliffs down almost to the water's edge I thought I saw movement beyond the tree-line. When I tried to locate it again I saw only wind movement. But I knew something was there, the way you do when you're hunting: you catch a movement without even being conscious of it, and suddenly you're certain of the presence of game. It's not so much intuition as recognition, the recognition of movements that has benefitted you before. But right now I didn't have a clue what to do next.

The beach was pretty clean where we were. No sticks, no rocks. I almost laughed at being caught in the open with only some limp seaweed in my hand.

'What did you laugh at?' Gillian asked with a smile, wanting to share the joke.

'I had a picture of the world on fire, no rules.'

'Really hilarious.' She shook her head in disbelief.

'I could exist in it,' I said. I had seen fire controlled. I had burned off paddocks with my father. A world in flames wouldn't have depressed me. There'd be excitement.

'The only way the world would burst into flame,' she said, 'is with atomic explosions. You don't even see the stuff that's killing you.'

She began to walk up to the tree-line. 'Hey!' I said. 'Don't leave me... Don't go up there!' I found a piece of kelp stalk as thick as a pick handle and walked up beside her. I had run through the bush up on this stretch of the point, and there was no way I was going to lose her, have her trapped in those walls of undergrowth. Some small rocks were clustered near the winter high tide mark; I picked up a few and hurled them into the bush nearby.

'What are you doing that for?' she asked, puzzled.

'I think we should be going back,' I said. But she registered the thick kelp as a weapon when I tapped it against my leg.

'What did you see?' she whispered.

'Nothing. I just want to go back.'

Minutes later the air exploded with flame. I caught the ripple of running orange as it threw out shadows, and then the whole point was up. We were three hundred metres from the closest part of the fire, but it took only moments for the searing heat to reach us. We were safe because the wind was angled away from us. It would only burn the twenty odd hectares of bush on the point.

'Should we run?' Gillian gasped.

'It's alright,' I said. 'We're OK. I've seen fires like this.' I was frightened though. Had the bastard wanted us to be barbecued on the beach, or was he trying to drive us somewhere? I had seen fire used in the rabbit plagues, and there was one thing I swore: never be trapped like a rabbit, always think before running. I could see flames reaching across the sand to the sea. 'Try burning that you bugger,' I said to myself.

'So now tell me how you knew someone was there,' Gillian said. We were walking backwards along the sand, our faces lit by the holocaust at the point. Above the bank of rippling flames there was a high snapping tongue of fire. Above that the sky was an inferno of colours entwining with the black smoke that followed the winds billowing out from the bush. I looked across at Gillian but her gaze had returned to the flame.

'I thought it was just nerves. I saw something, and then I decided I was just being stupid and overdramatising. So I pushed it out of my mind. I mean you don't expect stuff like this.' The raging colour over the point was a monument to destruction.

'He's insane,' she said. 'He's an old man that's missed out on something and he's going to get it any way he can. I can't really explain it. The feel of him was just repulsive. I knew I wasn't wrong about him.'

I thought of the bastard's madness, barely contained, close to Gillian, and I thought of all the animals I had stopped mid-stride with a headshot, and how I'd watched them skidding lifeless across the ground.

The fire was an outrageous move. If he could do that he was preparing for anything. I guessed he would have left the scene and run for the safety of the pub; or he was trailing us up there on the dunes. If he was still there rampaging, there was no way we could avoid him.

I looked up at the surf club, bathed in an orange glow. It was a small weatherboard building with a low tower over the roof intended for spotting sharks, but no one bothered. Beneath the tower to the east were the dressing-rooms and the rescue equipment; reels and stretchers were stacked on the west side. To the east of the building again, were the surfboard racks. It was a simple frame of shapely boards resting on loose pipes. Just last year we'd gone berserk in mock sword fights up there. The metallic sounds rang out over the dunes and infuriated the senior blokes who came down hard on us, shouting and then lecturing about responsibility. That time the fun was definitely only appreciated by the participants...

'I'll be back in a second,' I said.

She took my arm. 'Aaahhh, no you're not. I'm coming with you.'

'It'll be better for you here. If he got me you'd see him coming.'

'I don't want to see him coming. That's the last thing.'

'OK, but if he goes for us you run, right?'

'Right.'

We sprinted up the dune. By Christ the bastard would have to be fast to nail us. My legs simply wouldn't permit fatigue. We passed across the front of the club house and for a moment I thought of breaking in and having only a doorway to defend, but the bastard would burn it down. I slopped through the wet sand where the outside shower continued to leak, and grabbed for the pipes. The boards slid from them in bouncing thuds. Gillian grabbed a pipe and I banged hers against mine — the clanging to celebrate some sort of triumph — and we ran down the dunes again to the firm sand on the water's edge. If the farmer launched at us from the soft sand he would have some ground to make up. I laughed at Gillian hoping she would be affected by my hysterical enthusiasm. But she wasn't.

Gillian balanced her pipe over one shoulder and we set off around to the river. At the mouth we could hear cars along the main road. 'He wouldn't try anything here,' I said. But we still speeded up along the stretch of white sand to the car park. It was a relief to see the Kings, where by now a crowd had gathered. We dropped the pipes off at the edge of the gravel and I noted the spot.

I wanted to come back to them. We walked up to the crowd, and stood at the edge of it. The fire was visible high over the dunes and most of the onlookers were silent, reminded of the other fires taking their toll to the north, eating the guts out of the centre of the state. Those fires had already shown how easily a secure community could be ravaged.

Gillian took my hand. 'What do we do?'

'I suppose we tell someone.' But I was hesitant.

'We didn't really see who it was,' I said. 'Christ, we're only guessing.' I recalled the flitting shadow. No, it had been only a movement. She let go my hand.

'I'm leaving in the morning,' she declared. 'I'm not staying around here. I don't want to know about this sort of stuff.' She grasped my hand again. 'Come on.'

'Hey, I'm going to miss you,' I said as an obvious understatement. We walked across the road and up towards the guest house. I put my arm around her, quite naturally. I was almost surprised to find it there.

'You could come up to town with me,' she said. 'You could stay with my aunt and me.'

I didn't have time to second this wonderful plan, because the next moment she began to tremble.

'Are you OK?' I asked.

'No, I'm shaking, my knees won't keep still. But my mind is perfect!' And she touched her head with all her fingers spread.

An old ute rattled down the hill from the west and pulled up at the bowsers. It was the farmer. I felt an instant of hatred and then a coldness of intention. Gillian tried to head me off.

The farmer caught sight of me across the crowd and yelled out: 'That's him, that's the bastard! He started it! I saw him!'

'Fuck you!' I yelled, and my mouth was open the way

an athlete's is when he's been running under pressure and his nerve-ends cry out with the injustice of it. 'It was you, you brainless shithead, you cunt-featured moron, you tried to burn us!'

The farmer strode forward around the ute, his chest stuck out. 'You stupid bastard,' he said, stopping. 'You must be a bit cut or something. I'm telling the coppers.'

He turned back to his ute with a flourish of muscle activity, swung into the cabin and closed the door. Elated, I watched him drive off. Somehow, despite all evidence, it was as if he was running away. If he went to the police he was really opening a can of worms for himself. To come out in the open like that meant he was flushed from his cover of the ordinary, boisterous good bloke. But now he'd announced to the assembly that he had turned dobber.

I looked at Gillian. 'How about staying up with us tonight? I can sleep in my parents' room, or you could sleep in my bed and I'll sleep on the floor.' I grinned at her and shook my head as I saw her withdraw slightly, thinking it was an offer of bedding down with me. 'No, Jesus, nothing like that!'

'I'll come up with you now,' she said, '...for a while. Are you going to the police?'

'Hell no.'

'He will.'

'I don't think so. That was just for the crowd.'

'I think he will.'

'I'll talk to the judge then,' I said. 'He's a friend of my fathers.' It occurred to me that I had never run to an authority, especially one I held in a certain amount of contempt... but here I was, for Christsake, saying it...

We were about to cross the lane in front of the guest house when the ute sped up, then braked, its lights off and the dust rising like steam around it. The bastard's face was at the passenger window, threatening.

'You fuckin' Jew boy!' he screamed, choking in his rage. 'You think you're safe lording it up there with the rest of your fuckin' race, but we know where to get you!'

The rock I grabbed from the gravelled track was as big as a cricket ball. He was accelerating away when it took out his back window. He started to reverse, but when the second rock flew through the shattered glass and smashed his front window as well, he changed his mind and rocketed forward up onto the bitumen. A third rock careered off the passenger side door, and he pushed out the window with the fist. There was a spray of glass as he switched on his lights. I found myself on the main road watching his retreating tail light. Gillian took my hand. 'Come on,' she said. 'You need quietening down.' I grinned at her as we walked to the house.

'I've never been called a Jew before. It gave me a blast of something. I felt good!'

'I'm glad I'm going,' Gillian said. 'No one will be able to stop him.'

'Hell! He'll stop himself,' I said. 'He's about to explode.'

'And what about the people he'll take with him?'

My parents were out on the lawn at the guest house, watching the fire die down. They were mingling with the staff and some neighbours who had walked up the rise for a better view.

'Dad... Mum, this is Gillian Blyton.'

'Oh,' my mother said. 'I've seen you before; you're at the shop.' My father shook her hand. Gillian smiled and greeted them both. Her easy, straightforward manner made me conscious of my own lack of spontaneity.

'Look, Dad,' I began. 'We've got something to tell you. We were along at the point when the fire started.'

'Jim!' my mother cut in. 'You didn't...'

'No. We didn't. But you wouldn't believe what we've seen... been through. There's a bloody madman out there.'

I told them briefly what had happened; that I'd seen a figure moving in the bush and that we'd had a run-in with the farmer. My father walked over to the judge and they stood talking. The judge nodded a few times and then looked across to us in surprise. He moved over to the verandah steps and stood on the lowest one. Then my father waved us over. The judge was now the same height as my father, and because Gillian and I were standing on the gravel path we were much shorter than they were. They both seemed more at ease with this arrangement.

'Are you sure you had nothing to do with this?' the judge asked in a stern voice. It was so phoney and sententiousness I almost laughed. Schoolmasters managed to produce such tones from the meaner parts of their minds.

'Of course we didn't bloody do it,' I snapped. I stopped there — anything else would have triggered a flow of abuse. Already the words felt like verbal missiles in my mind. I coughed and kicked at the gravel, focussing my eyes beyond the judge and my father. I tried to blank them out of my vision completely, to be conscious only of their words.

'Could you identify this man?' the judge asked. 'Did you see him clearly enough? Did the fire begin immediately after you'd seen him?'

I looked at Gillian: what have we got here?

'It was a movement,' I said. 'I caught a movement and knew it must be something.'

The judge coughed as if he was trying to attract attention: 'Humph!'

'Did he tell you he'd seen something?' he asked Gillian.

'No, I only realised he'd seen something when he picked up a piece of thick kelp.'

'You mean he didn't tell you immediately?'

'No,' she said.

The judge stepped down from the verandah. So he didn't

feel threatened any longer? His head was thrown back so far he looked like a bantam rooster. He glanced at me with severity, but I was immune to that sort of thing now. After all, I'd been glowered at by so many schoolmasters over the years, and just now I'd had to confront a madman's plan to annihilate me. Compared with that the judge was a pushover.

'This is all supposition on your part?' the judge accused.

'I suppose so,' I answered, 'but he *has* threatened us, and everybody in the guest house...'

The judge chuckled patronisingly. 'If everybody who had issued a threat came before my court there'd be no one walking the streets.'

He was bent more on scoring points in this court house by the sea, than raising his head to witness the fire that had destroyed the point.

The judge smiled benignly at the hopeless idiots standing around him and touched Gillian's arm. 'Off with you,' he said. 'It'll be taken into good account that you came to me with your story.'

Mum had been standing a few steps away. I went up to her and told her that Gillian would be staying in my room. She seemed slightly shocked.

'Your mate the judge has no idea what's happening. Gillian's been attacked by this bloke before, and she needs somewhere safe. I'll sleep on the floor in your room.'

My mother was nothing if not quick. 'We'll get her a room here,' she said. 'That will be alright.' She smiled at Gillian who was full of thanks.

My room seemed much smaller with Gillian there. I hadn't been conscious of its size before. It had a high ceiling to combat the heat, but with this summer's scorching, it still had the warmth of an oven's after-heat. I smelt burning eucalyptus; the smoke from the fire must have circled back in small amounts from the ocean and seeped in here. Outside

I hadn't noticed the bitterness of the smoke at all.

'Well aaaah,' I began, 'you can shower and everything here. I'll get you a towel.' Gillian looked at me and laughed. It excited me. It was a laugh of conspiracy, a laugh of welcome. I put my arms around her. Together we seemed to create a real energy. It was something special and we knew it. Her body was firm, moulded, and her skin was soft. I kissed her hesitantly. She showed me in an instant how easy and enjoyable it was. She laughed again and pulled away when she realised how eager I was.

'You'll be more relaxed after a shower and something to eat,' I said, in an effort to reverse the roles.

When I came back from the kitchen with some egg and lettuce sandwiches and slices of lemon meringue pie, she had showered, washed her hair and was sitting up in bed with her shirt on.

'I feel like a kept woman,' she said.

'That's good,' I said.

'What do you mean?'

'You must feel amenable.'

'I didn't say I liked the feeling.'

'We'll have to follow that up then.'

'I think a kept woman must feel trapped.'

I handed her a plate with sandwiches and pie. 'But it's me who's trapped. I'm waiting on you.'

'Only for one reason.'

'What's that then?'

'My favours.'

'You are old-fashioned.'

She giggled, suppressing outright laughter. 'If I was old fashioned I wouldn't be sitting in this bed.'

'Unless you were an old-fashioned woman of favours.'

We ate the food rather hurriedly and then, worried that I might muck up the move on her I was planning, I walked to the window rather aimlessly. I leaned on the window frame watching the guttering of odd flames from the now darkening point.

'Some people would reckon that was adventure out there,' I said.

'There's better adventure,' she said suggestively. When I looked at her she smiled openly. I walked to the bed and sat beside her. I grabbed her body awkwardly, but the overall feeling was right. I was not pretending I was a great lover and therefore the soft lust that overwhelmed me was OK. She moved down in the bed slightly and I thought, there's some nice thighs down there alright.

'Your parents might come in,' she said.

'They'll knock,' I said, not caring where the smoothness of her touch might end. 'We're not doing anything anyway.'

'Anything wrong,' she whispered. 'I feel safe here.'

I could feel an irregular rhythm to my breathing. I didn't want to pant. My mother knocked a few minutes later and we sprang apart as if we had indeed been doing something wrong. I felt ridiculous, and trapped. 'Come in,' I said. I was leaning casually on the window frame again. It was a minute or two before I could turn and face her, but she was looking at Gillian and didn't notice my peculiar manner.

'You're in luck, they have a spare room for you Gillian,' my mother announced. 'How are you feeling now? It's been something of an ordeal for you.'

Gillian smiled, sweet with innocence. 'I'm fine now,' she said.

My mother continued. 'They tell me he was something of a war hero and that the locals put up with him.'

'After something like this?'

'No, not at all. They don't believe he'd do that sort of thing.'

Gillian looked at me, miming hopelessness with a fleeting grimace.

'They know he's wild,' my mother explained. 'I suppose you could say they are just tolerant, I think that would be it.'

'Like hell!' I laughed. 'They love his bloody antics. *All* his antics. If he was a politician they'd vote for him on the spot.'

'Not these days,' my mother said. 'Politics is becoming very serious. The fat little Russian seems to have set off the alarm bells. I think you'd need to be squeaky clean.'

'He's the sort of bastard that would persecute someone whether he was a commo or not,' I said. 'If he thought you were a commo as well as a Jew, he'd be round the bend. He's threatened us all up here as it is.'

'What do you mean?' my mother asked.

'You know, he'd remember the Jews up at the guest house, that sort of stuff. I mean its all bullshit.'

'That's obviously how the locals see it,' my mother said. I looked at Gillian to see if she wanted to tell her story, but she didn't seem inclined to.

'He's a madman,' I said. 'And I know — I can't prove it — that it *was* him on the point.'

'I can understand you're upset,' my mother reasoned, and she made it sound like a weakness. That made me wilder, but also more cautious about exposing my anger. 'Not quite as upset as *he* is I think.' I said.

'But he's a madman, dear.' I didn't know where she had discovered the 'dear' stuff. Perhaps she was conforming to her image of the protective mother because Gillian's presence made her uneasy about her own role with me.

She moved over to the bedside table and slid the plates together. 'I'll just take these back,' she said. 'Are you sure there is nothing else you want?' she smiled at me before shutting the door. I was astounded. Evidently, it was only a matter of my having a relationship with an approved person outside the family, for my status within it to be somewhat improved. Or was it simply that my mother recognised the trauma of Gillian's ordeal? As she closed the door, I went back to sit on the bed.

'Your mother doesn't look Jewish,' Gillian said.

'She's not. Her side of the family was French. Her mother was the daughter of a French army officer who married a Scottish doctor and stayed here.'

'Toooo much!' Gillian exclaimed. 'I didn't know we had those sort of combinations in Australia. You're not Jewish then,' she added. 'Jewish blood only flows from the mother.'

I laughed. 'How do they know?'

'It's belief. You should know it all.'

'It's all bullshit,' I said. 'It doesn't affect me at all. Anyway, I don't mind being Jewish. Their religion is just as wrong as anybody else's.' I walked over to the mirror and hammed up an act of looking at myself in profile, turning my nose from side to side. 'I thought they might be wrong,' I said looking across at her, 'but the strain is definitely there.'

'And your father?' she asked.

'My great grandfather escaped a pogrom in Poland as a boy and came here late last century, when Jews still had to get permission to marry from the rabbi of London. His son married an Irish blacksmith's daughter. You know, coming over the equator her family were told by the sailors to put on more clothes to keep out the heat and the sailors laughed at the dumbness of the expiring potato eaters! So in a way the Irish have been persecuted here as much as the Jews!'

During those moments there was a heightened friendliness between us. I could never have joked with my parents about being a Jew. Their racism extended to thinking that Jews were a superior race.

I wanted that affection I had with Gillian to be developed, but I had no idea how to take it further. It was a condition

I knew little about; alliances at boarding school were based on whether support could be expected from an individual, or whether two people had the same riotous sense of humour. With her I could sense an aura that I couldn't really identify although it had a feel of gentle concern. Looking down at her again, I imagined that the softness of her concealed body must be a delight. I would have liked to see her thighs, naked, astride a horse. I was addicted to masturbation and often imagined thighs astride a lot of things.

'You're lucky to have parents like that,' she said.

'You think they're good?' I asked doubtfully, but then their unquestioning acceptance of Gillian's presence had to be significant.

Two hours later, restless and confused, I was walking on the beach. The sand was slightly chilled as it squeaked under my feet. I had been unable to sleep; images of Gillian, now ensconced and sleeping in a room just down the hall from mine, had been changing with the pace of my heart. I had tried knocking gently on her door, but either she was sleeping soundly or didn't wish to have my presence forced on her, and I gave it away.

Alright, I told myself, be cool. Anything but cool, I had let myself out the side door off the hall and walked down to the ocean. There under a night sky the sea was moving in a massive and regular rhythm that suited the summer. I walked down the dunes, across the beach and into the water. My imagination had a complete picture of a shark moving slowly over the ripples of sand, sinister, effortless, guided by instinct alone: a fearful machine capable of harvesting an over-abundance of protein. Fuck that, I thought.

The previous year, as we had trained in a surfboat for the coming surf carnivals, the dull grind under a scorching sky had been enlivened by the fin of a large shark that surfaced beside us. I prayed that the slight breeze fretting the surface of the water would remain with us. I had a horror of glimpsing the creature that had been created for work at the end of the line.

'Jesus, let's get the bastard,' the sweep oarsman yelled, challenging himself and frightening his crew.

'Let the fucker swim away,' I yelled, suggesting we should go easy on him. As if we had a hope of capturing him anyway. To suggest we didn't would have driven the mad sweep oarsman to renewed efforts. In his action-position, using split-second timing to take the boat on or off a wave, he had an ingrained habit of taking a chance. To ask him for a decision on whether we should chase a shark or not was similar to asking a soldier to negotiate a peace.

For an absurd moment on that boat I had a desire to run across the surface to the shore. Obviously a mind that could conjure such mystical moments was vulnerable to a concept like this. Luckily I remembered in time that only one man had ever done it with success.

We chased that fuckin' shark until our wind was tight and hot in our chests and our forearms were numb, incapable of doing anything but hold an oar. Before disappearing it made one pass down the side of our boat as the breeze dropped. It seemed to wrinkle its nose like a soft puppet and a cloud of filth belched from the mouth. Amongst the filth was a yellow label in a foreign language.

'It's been out in the shipping channel gobbling wog food,' said the sweep, confident any joke would go down well with a junior crew. I had to restrain the need to take my oar and beat on the water over the creature's head.

Be cool, I had told myself, it might just go away. And eventually it did.

Its disappearance was unsensational. The fin submerged in an easy glide. That was it. Nothing! It was possible it had never existed. I thought about that ocean cleaner for a long time after: I had thought of it as the ultimate death machine, and then I understood that it was really only a predatory mouse compared to humans with a lust to kill. Generals clawed their way to the top of their profession for the power to decide how thousands of other people died. They did it for their country of course, but how many people would kill without being urged by those at the top who wanted the excitement of war? Frightened men could make decisions to have others kill for them. What were their feelings? What were their excitements? Were they so proud of their power? Or did it mean they were something less than human? I'd love one of those bloodthirsty urgers to meet a grey eminence on an ocean floor. Would they fight it with the enthusiasm they expected of their men? Or would their blood lust dissolve along with their frightened shit?

Now I thought I could kill the farmer without inhibition. He'd be no more problem for me than slapping a wild boar in the head with a bullet that travelled with the weight of tonnes. I felt the anticipation of catching the farmer in mid-stride. Whomph! And the bastard would spin in the air only to hit the ground like a bag of spuds. It was fascinating that one part of me existed with the knowledge that I could think of slaughtering a human being, while simultaneously, I functioned as a normal social machine. I lay down to contemplate the feelings that ran with those thoughts.

I woke to sounds I couldn't immediately recognise. It's the way you wake on a farm to unusual movements of animals. Your mind struggles for the sounds that will identify the crisis. There was no bellowing now, or thuds of bulls fighting, nor the high screams of stallions, so I kept listening. I was having trouble focussing on my surroundings.

The voices were furtive and tense. After a few moments I crawled towards the sounds and recognised the grunts and threats of a man.

'Stay still you fuckin' bitch,' the man demanded. And then there were slaps. I seemed to be moving quite slowly and my vision tunnelled as if I was looking through a pipe. The man was beside the woman in a clearing of sand. He was slapping her thighs from side to side. He didn't seem to care whether they parted or not. The blows became harder and the woman was tossed about like a puppet. Suddenly she threw herself into a clenched position. I broke through the scrub and my vision cleared.

'You disgusting pig!' Rachel yelled.

The farmer turned to meet me, and as I hit out with a lunging fist I knew I had jumped without balance. My force was gone. And then he hit me. The punches caused no pain and were like bumps from a pillow, but I couldn't raise my arms to defend myself. Why was I feeling no pain? My hand gripped his shirt and when he punched again the rag was torn from his back. I was suspended in blackness and felt myself falling.

For some time it was quiet. When I moved my hands, spreading the fingers, I felt the coolness of the sheets. I was comfortable so I continued to lie there. It seemed I had craved for a long time the fatigue I now felt. I was satisfied with myself and I was alive. Furtively I moved my toes. I could feel them work. Again I lay still. There was a soft movement beside the bed and I opened my eyes. The nurse smiled down at me. She had a wonderful face.

'I see you're with us,' she smiled. 'You've been away for some time.'

'How long?'

'A few hours anyway.'

'Is everything alright?'

'Everything but some abrasions on your face and a few broken ribs.'

'I can't feel them.'

'You will when you move.'

I decided not to move.

'What happened?'

'Well, where do I start? He ran off did Mr Larra, shot through into the hills. They're looking for him now, but I doubt they'll find him.'

'Is Rachel hurt?'

'She's fine. He took her from the bathroom, you know. Right out of the guest house and nobody heard him.'

'Was anybody else hurt or anything?'

'No,' she said, placing a thermometer in my mouth.

## CHAPTER 5

Gillian ran down to the water, a dark nymph dancing in the shallows that dazzled with sun. The two nights I had spent under observation in hospital I had dreamed of her. She was pursued by men, idolised by men, and when she stood before them on the white boxes they had brought for her to stand on, they gazed at her in silence. When she refused to descend among them as they requested, they turned nasty. They began to grab at her but she raised her arms and pulled herself into the foliage of a tree. I was filled with admiration. I had woken from those dreams pleased with the overwhelming commitment I had to her, and it didn't disappear with the reality of the morning.

She dived beneath a wave that broke softly over her. It was a small wave and within moments she was up and striding through hip-deep water, leaning forward slightly against the flow, her forearms moving with the rhythm of her body as if they were pushing through the surface and not the air above it.

Gillian had visited me in hospital and sat on my bed. The sight of her hips distracted me and I touched her knee quite casually; she didn't withdraw it. Beneath the bed clothes I became firmly erect. When she left she kissed me on the lips and laughed. There was companionship in her touch, along with the eroticism. I wasn't sure whether it was gratitude, concern or love. But as they were mistaken about my ribs being broken I was certain I was close to discovering.

The farmer, Dave Larra, had gone bush to hide, the police said, in the Otway ranges. He had taken Rachel from the bathroom of the guest house and carried her, his hand over her mouth, down the corridor and across the road to the dunes. Hans had been asleep when she left the room, and the guest house had been quiet. The bastard had it all his own way until I blundered through the bush. Rachel said he had only run because he thought I was the first in a concerted rush. I was grateful he had some imagination.

The search for Larra began with considerable enthusiasm, there was even talk of using an aeroplane to spot him, but the fires had flared again in the Wimmera and the plane had been needed there. A plane would have been useless anyway in the search for the farmer; the Otway forests were dense and vast. I suspected the police only wanted to impress on people the sophistication of their methods.

The police had driven down the fire-fighting tracks into the Otways. They were well marked on maps but in fact only extended a few miles into the foothills, then stopped. Larra's old mother said he had fled in the ute, so the authorities became firmly convinced he had fled interstate. To believe that was to be positive. Not to believe it was to have either failure, or an immense amount of work, staring them in the face.

I knew the bastard was in those hills. Why run when even on the coldest summer nights he could sit in the open and watch the ocean flooding the coast? If he hunted or fished, a rifle shot would blend with the crack of the waves; there would be no problems until the winter months. But more than this, I knew he was a man who lived for revenge. He would think he had been hard done by and that it should be the tourists who had no right to be in the area. He would hate to be the fugitive in his own territory. His sole pre-occupation as he fumed through the dense scrub would be thoughts of revenge. It seemed to me that if he were any sort of farmer he would be committed to his stock, and I guessed he would emerge from the bush each evening along with the kangaroos with a taste for pasture, just to check his animals.

But what do you tell police whose equipment places them beyond the range of the small search? They liked thrashing their radio cars along the small dirt tracks, muttering code calls into their microphones. They wanted to conceive of crime on the American scale. You read a great deal about people fleeing interstate to avoid detection. And so many criminals did. The police wanted glamour and crime conceived on the grand scale, and so they got it mostly. However all crookedness begins in a small way, and they weren't looking for the tiny watersheds. Common sense they told the judge, said that he had fled interstate; they had seen no sign of him. Nobody had any thoughts about a lurking madman. I couldn't understand how I seemed to know about the obsessive feelings and the actions of the man, when the police so easily gave him credit for being rational. Perhaps my parents had been right to send me away boarding. I'd been too long living with animals. And yet I knew there were plenty like me who laughed at the veneer of civilisation, and understood that the capacity to imagine the most outlandish experiences and circumstances was in fact no more than evoking in your own head the actions or ideas of other people.

At night I gazed from the verandah up into the hills, wondering when the first signs of him would arrive. By the end of the week the search had been scaled down to asking for reports of strangers drifting out of the bush to local stores or pubs, or for unusual sightings; and yet the holidaymakers at Anglecrest were assured that there was an intensive nationwide hunt for the man. The judge told us he had been assured that there would be no rest until they found him. Quizzed on the lack of visible police in the area the judge said they were needed in the fire areas to the north.

And while I was waiting for signs of him, my anger was being neutralised by Gillian. I was feverishly in love. It was tearing me about so much I wondered whether the feeling was simply an indulgent habit I wanted to prolong. Any thoughts of Larra entered a mind that was feverish with the presence of Gillian, and as I could only operate at extremes of the emotional scale, my hatred of him was complete. I was glad I had pilfered an old four-ten shotgun I had found on the top of the tool cupboard in the workroom behind the guest house. Les had neglected it badly. The barrels had been filthy and rust-pitted on the outside, but I had cleaned it and bought a packet of cartridges for it. Not that it was a great weapon — a four-ten would have difficulty stopping a hare forty metres out. But as I became more absorbed with Gillian I knew that if I hadn't lifted the weapon on the first day out of hospital I would have neglected to arm myself at all.

We had become intimately concerned for our own and

each other's pleasure. Not that we were fucking, but I was dizzy with the variety of possibilities each time we were together. And I imagined at the time that if every kid of my age could experience so much outright enjoyment in a relationship there would be little chance that he could be persuaded to leave it for more aggressive activities.

At dinner one night I was given clear evidence that my parents liked Gillian.

She and I had spent the day in the shallows at the river mouth. It was all I could do to float there in a warm salt solution. And Gillian played with me, her body as smooth as a seal's. Occasionally her brown face would emerge dripping in front of me and we would caress with slippery mouths.

My parents had been in Melbourne for the day and they announced that they had been to see Gillian's aunt who had agreed that if she wanted, Gillian could stay for another fortnight. Gillian had written alerting her to the fact that she was no longer working at the Kings but was staying with a friend. No one had told me however, and the agreement was announced with all the laughs and nudges of friends in conspiracy. My parents were now determined to have good times.

Rachel wasn't interested in discussing the night she had been abducted and assaulted. I thought the fact that I had been flattened in a bid to save her might be a stimulant there, but it was as if the whole event was of no consequence to her. One morning I sat beside her on the canvas chairs in the shade of a willow, but we didn't speak of the incident at all.

She spoke to Gillian about it one evening during coffee and told her she thought I had been courageous. When Gillian told me this I said it wasn't true, that I had only attacked the bastard because I personlly had felt cornered in some way and had been so frightened that I had been forced to follow through. Naturally I had been tempted to claim courage, but if you claim things that aren't true you often find yourself out on a limb somewhere, with no way to crawl back to reality. This had occurred to me while I listened to the Squadron Leader giving evidence of his own bravery. He had said my father couldn't discuss the war because he hadn't been there, hadn't participated. My old man had argued that if you had seen violence, or been frightened, your imagination supplied the rest. The Squadron Leader had laughed, dismissing my father's courage and emphasising his own. My old man had been angry. He asked the Squadron Leader if he had been on the ground when the bombs he had dropped had landed. 'No', the Squadron Leader had replied. 'In a way then,' my father suggested, 'your knowledge of war is rather one-sided.'

Obviously there was plenty of room for violent dissension amongst the guests. Both my father and the Squadron Leader volunteered their help to the police. I had laughed at the thought of Arthur Waterhouse calling on their wives offering life insurance policies. Luckily the police wouldn't hear of civilians joining the hunt.

One evening Gillian and I were talking in the car about what we intended to do at university. At least she was, for I had no interest in doing anything at the university. Whatever I did there would be completely irrelevant to the way I progressed, or so I thought. I was actually wondering how I could slide my hand along her leg and under her dress as if it was the most natural thing in the world. My mind therefore was roaming freely and creatively. Behind her was the solid darkness of the foothills, and for an instant I saw them alight, in flame . . . but when the moment passed I said to myself, no, that was the reflection of the headlights of a passing car, or a sudden flare of light from the verandah. I was busily trying to explain it all away, when my mind concluded for me, without my bidding, that this was the sign that Dave Larra would burn the hills, and the town with it. What was more natural for an infected mind? He could engineer his own disappearance at the same time.

I told Gillian what I thought.

She didn't agree. 'Stuff him,' she said. She was beginning to use my style of language. She claimed she had sworn only rarely before she met me and in every snatch of conversation there was a curse waiting to get out.

'The bastard's out there,' I said.

'I'm not obsessed with him,' she said. 'I don't think you should be. He's just a sick case.'

'I'm not obsessed,' I said. 'Not in an unreasonable way. But I don't think it's the end of him.' Often I had let the chance to be prophetic slip by. Later, when the events I had predicted occurred, I was disappointed that I hadn't persisted. I slid my hand along the outside of her thigh to the elastic line of her knickers. I pretended it was an idle caress. Her dress had moved upwards with my hand and her legs were lithe and vulnerable.

'I'm sorry,' she said. 'I don't feel like it.' She held my hand on her thigh and looked at me as if she knew I would understand. I removed it slowly and looked understanding.

'Is that alright?' she asked.

'Sure,' I said.

She let her light dress remain where my exploring hand had taken it. Her legs were superb and completely distracting.

'It's just that something is blocking me. I don't know if it's something I have to say, or not.'

'I like talking,' I said. 'I really like talking to you, and listening to you.'

'Later then,' she said. 'I promise.' So that was being on a promise.

'I've been talking to Rachel,' she said. I had seen them thoroughly absorbed over coffee on several occasions. 'I told her all about the farmer. She told me that that sort of thing is really completely meaningless and that although it was best to only do the things you want, if you are actually forced, not to let it destroy you, harm you. Be in control, but if it's beyond your control don't be upset or feel guilty, even if your body keeps working against what you want. And only think about it for as long as you need to; don't carry it on.'

'I think that's probably right.' If she wanted me to take it further I couldn't.

'The thing that happened to me was sort of interesting, thinking back on it, that is. I mean under other circumstances it might have been exciting, but the girl needs to be in control of it all, otherwise she could be hurt.'

I speculated on whether that was an invitation to be aggressive or not, but I decided I didn't know enough and that if I felt it was only going to be blundering, it would turn out bad.

'Do you mean, having a few men could be exciting, or is it the roughness that's exciting? "Firmness" I mean.'

She giggled. 'I couldn't handle too many men, although perhaps I meant that. I don't know.'

I resisted the temptation to confuse her further by grabbing her, although I was excited and hot. Just listen, I told myself, there's plenty of time and I really only want to do what she would enjoy. But without thinking I reached beneath the tiny apron of the dress and touched her pants and her cunt.

'Oh,' she said, surprised. She looked at me, dropping the hand she had lifted to prevent further exploration. I stroked the pants as I watched her face. Her eyes were in shadow but I was sure she ran a tongue between her lips.

'Do you like that?' I asked. She nodded yes.

'God, I do,' I said.

'Really,' she said with a quick breath. 'I thought you might.'

We talked like that as I ran my hand over the cloth. working my fingers under the elastic I leaned forward to see her cunt, to be sure of what my fingers were doing. The inside of her thighs tensed slightly.

'I don't know if I like this,' she said and I looked up into a hesitant face.

'Don't stop it just because you're not sure,' I reasoned. 'See if you do.' She nodded and I trailed my fingers back and forth along the lips.

'Here comes your mother,' she said and flicked her dress over her legs. I sat back and we looked suitably casual when my mother tapped on the window behind me. I turned with a rather horrid grin on my face but she didn't notice.

'I wondered where you were,' she smiled. I wound down the window.

'We're just talking. We'll be in in a minute I think.' She became uneasy and I thought the open window may have allowed the atmosphere in the car to escape.

'Yes I think that would be a good idea.' She looked around as if the hostility of the night was reason enough. 'I wanted to know where you were before we went to bed.'

Gillian hadn't said a word and I looked at her when my mother walked off. Her face was composed but her eyes were gleaming. I pulled back her dress and I saw she hadn't moved. I ran one finger over the hair and she shuddered slightly.

'I can't stand this,' she said.

'You don't like it?'

'No, I do. It's too good. It's almost like tickling.' I parted the lips and leaned forward to kiss her.

'I know you like it,' I said, although the comment was already pointless, but it was an intimate reinforcement on my part. My fingers entered the warm moistness and she breathed, 'Oh, this is not fair.'

'Don't worry,' I said, although it was not a considered opinion.

## CHAPTER 6

When the fires started I knew the farmer had come back for more attention. I sensed he would have been bored, trailing through the back blocks and losing his identity to the small straggling gums that carpeted the low ranges sloping to the sea. He was the sort of bastard who needed people to bounce off, annoy, taunt, ridicule. It would be unacceptable for them to have forgotten him, to have pulled out. While the car lights and the pursuers' night lights were there for him to gloat over he was someone important, running on adrenalin. With his pursuers away in the northern fires, he was stimulated to play. The first fires were small but I saw a pattern to them: they looked random enough but they were more to the north of the town, and if there hadn't been a respite from the northerlies, the town would have been fighting for its existence.

When I told my father that I thought the fires were being lit by the farmer, he laughed, saying I could be right, and walked off to tell the judge. I hadn't really needed to tell my father; I had seen him down at the tennis court, looking up over the guest house at the smoke in the north, but I suppose his son telling him, someone who knew less of the bush than he did, shamed him into doing something about it. Farmers know a revenge fire. In all the time they live in their area, they absorb the feuds, their implications and their degrees of seriousness. They watch not only for the patterns of fire, but also of water. If levee banks are destroyed, or water re-routed, they know where it has all come from. They might have heard only a word on sale day in town but if it fits the jigsaw they build their picture and act in a way that won't bring them into conflict with the potential combatants. And so I knew my father was calculating the odds that it was our farmer who was responsible. He would have had to take into account that there were animosities he knew nothing about, but the right conclusion wasn't really hard to come by because no one starts a series of fires without expecting to draw a great deal of anger and vengeful emotion.

I had listened at the dinner table to talk of things that had got out of hand. The result of all this was that my father took the judge and the Squadron Leader for a car tour up around where the fires had been lit. I asked to go but they wouldn't have felt serious with me tagging along, despite the fact that I knew all about the bastard. However, I had got emotional, saying that he could only be stopped in one way. My father thought this was ridiculous and was pretty short with me. I wondered what they would do if they came across him, not realising at the time that they had no intention of doing so, and that if they had seen him in the distance they'd have left him there.

I hung around the guest house until they returned. I stayed with Gillian in the small block next to the guest house. The paddock had high fences on two sides and distant trees on the other two; the grass where we lay talking was high enough to conceal us. We couldn't keep our hands off each other while we were alone. We'd talk for a time until eagerness dampened the conversation and then I'd touch her arm or lean over and kiss her neck. It seemed to me that nobody had made such movements before. The feelings were so fresh. I couldn't imagine that they had been felt by anyone else. She often smiled at me in a welcoming way which dispelled uncertainty.

So I didn't see them until much later that evening. They were so full of aggression that they had left the door of the judge's room open, thus preventing any explosive arguments. It seemed the judge was rejecting the arguments of my father and the Squadron Leader.

'Just because a fire begins away from the roadway it is no evidence that it has been deliberately lit,' I heard the judge say.

'That is exactly the point,' my father replied. 'It is rare to have accidental fires away from roadways, especially a whole bloody series of them. It's the cigarette out the window or broken bottles that start them. A whole series like that would be impossible unless there was lightning or something.'

'Makes sense to me,' the Squadron Leader said in a most supportive and authoritative voice.

The judge spilt his glass of whisky as he slammed it down on the table. 'It's ridiculous for you to contemplate making such a judgement.' He picked his glass up and walked with it to the window. 'Although it would be in order to make a report of your suspicions.' What else did my father wish him to do? I wondered.

'Did you see anything?' I asked from the doorway. No one seemed inclined to answer me or even acknowledge me. 'Any sign of him Dad?' I asked specifically.

'No,' he said rather absently. 'No Jim.'

'Sounds uneventful,' I said sarcastically. It was clear that they were waiting for me to move down the hall before they began arguing again. Obviously I had only heard a small piece of the evidence. Fuck them, I thought, they're only ditherers anyway. I'd seen adults argue themselves out of action many times before. My own feelings were so firmly entrenched I hardly needed to refer to them anymore. They were there as a solid base from which to launch myself. I also had that knowledge of an impending confrontation. The time would come and I didn't need to plan for it. I had been tempted to force the issue and roam about on that line where the fires had been started, but that was exactly what Larra was expecting. Not me necessarily, but somebody poking around. And I would have been conceding that he could draw me on. There was a madman giggling away up there.

Later I tackled my father about the things they had seen. They had seen something, he told me, a figure, but he could have been, as the judge had maintained, just another sightseer. They didn't really know what the farmer looked like and they hadn't been close enough to bring back a description of the figure.

'Why didn't you ask me then?' I said, turning away. But I was just 'the overacting adolescent', as we were described in those days. The bastards didn't know what they were in for in the ensuing decades, as they gave up all semblance of knowing anything beyond the perceptions their parents had passed down to them. I was beginning to understand that I was part of a movement away from the dependence on knowledge that parents were alleged to possess. I could sense it in the films, in the music and in myself. Parents couldn't relate to the questions that kids wanted answers to. I knew for myself now that all their talking and concern couldn't even begin to convey the magic of touching another person you wanted. It was as if they had given up on that too.

The feeling of being menaced added something to my relationship with Gillian. Our moments together were becoming hotter. I think on my part there was an edge of jealousy: a desperate urge to reach her emotionally to the degree the farmer had. I didn't necessarily want her fearful, but at times I thought that it might do in place of anything else.

We talked of Rachel's experiences, at least I did, trying to discover if there was something in certain people that attracted them to those horrific conditions. I found that Gillian and Rachel had talked far more than I was aware of. Gillian was fascinated by the other woman.

'That bastard gave you something of a thrill, didn't he?' I asked with barely a hint of accusation.

'I mentioned it before,' she said. 'I don't really know.'

'You don't want to look at it too closely?'

'Why are you so interested?'

'Weeeell,' I began. 'It fascinates me as well.' I tried a laugh.

'Rachel says that often you just can't take anything for granted, that you can't predict what will happen, that you can't use the traditional guidelines to find out about yourself. I think I know what she means.'

I was astonished. 'You mean you were discussing what I've just been talking about?'

'Of course.'

'So you wouldn't mind a lot of blokes feeling you up?'

'Would you mind a lot of girls feeling you up?'

I had missed that. I laughed. 'My imagination seems to have failed me,' I said.

'Would you like to think about me with other boys?'

I pushed her down on the sand. I think I was a little too rough with her because she asked if I could slow down. 'Just stroke me gently,' she said. I was beyond anything but instinct and I think she caught my rush; as my body began convulsing against her thigh, she moved it for me.

When I had subsided onto the sand she looked across at me. 'I need you to help me,' she said.

'Take your shorts off,' I said feeling a control I hadn't even looked for. She sat up arranging a towel beneath her, unbuttoned her shorts, and with a look that was almost asking for permission, slipped them down her legs.

'Take those off too,' I said, and she looked like she might cry.

'I don't want to,' she said.

'You've had them off before,' I told her, although now wasn't quite the same. She slipped one leg out of her pants and then pulled them up against her. I pulled them down her thighs again. 'I don't want to, you know,' she said. 'I mean I really don't.'

'I'm not going to,' I said. 'It's whatever you want. If you say you don't want to, I won't.'

'I don't want to,' she said.

I thought of all the excuses and explanations, but finally I didn't want to force her to do anything. All this confusion would eventually sort itself out. I knew I could take her, force her, and there would be no real recriminations, but I didn't want to be the domineering thug. And the fear seemed to increase her passion as she heaved under my intense fingers. While we caught our breaths on the baking sand, I contemplated my disparate feelings, knowing that if I thought through them as I lay there, I would eventually understand why sex flooded the body with such conflicting emotions: tenderness and savagery. I knew that somehow, in the play of our bodies, one with the other, could be found all the secrets of love and hate. And the worst of it was that everybody approached the play with their own ideas of how it should be.

When I followed her across the road as evening came, I watched her legs and her swaying hair, and I knew she was someone I could sacrifice most things for. Drawing level with her, I hugged her with one arm and ran my hand up the leg of her shorts to hold her shapely buttock.

'You're insatiable!' she laughed.

'I sure am,' I said holding her movement. It felt like

touching the skin of a smooth-pelted animal. To have this girl for a moment would make you want more. I began to see things the way Farmer Larra would. I wondered if there had been other incidents she hadn't told me about. Perhaps he had been in a similar position to myself. I looked down at her, but her sheer beauty inhibited any doubts. I would believe her because I wanted to. Something this good didn't occur very often and might never again.

That night in the dining-room we ate well. We were full of secrets, but managed to carry on a normal conversation with my parents. At one point I stunned her when I bent to pick up my table napkin from the floor and ran my hand along the bottom of her thighs and between her legs. She stared at me as if I had captured her. I looked at my parents boldly, without meeting their eyes, and laughed a little too wildly.

'You know it's really peculiar that we're sitting here so normally, behaving as though nothing has happened, and yet we know that not far away is a maniac. I mean, he really wants to burn us, and we're doing nothing about it.'

I had launched myself into this spiel as a way of distracting my parents from my moves towards Gillian at the table, but the conclusion I had improvised in my little speech knocked me about. It seemed I had stumbled onto the secret of how the human race behaved when faced with danger: stay as still as a hunted animal and hope that you'll survive. But that was exactly the reverse of how we had always been told the human race survived. Animals might behave like that, but humans were supposed to confront and solve their problems.

'Rachel said something like that,' Gillian said, and looked at me strangely, as though I might have been eavesdropping.

My mother looked as if she didn't really understand,

and my father looked down at his meal and said, yes that was right, and that we really hadn't learned much from the lessons of history.

'We're comfortable here,' he pronounced. 'I think that's probably the criterion we live by. I know I don't want to leave, and I'm not sure why not. Does anybody else want to leave?' He looked around expectantly. None of us did. He was avoiding the issue, as well as being illogical. It was pathetic.

After dinner, Gillian and I headed off to the surf club dance. It was held at the RSL hall where there were pictures three nights a week on the big screen, and a dance in aid of the new surf club once a week. Dances had always frightened me, and the previous Christmas, despite being an active winner of trophies for the club, I had never made it to one. I had hovered in the area though, watching through the trees at the girls in their summer dresses, their long legs inspiring me later to a frenzy of masturbation. The smell of perfume on summer nights mixed with the wafts of suntan lotion and the hot metal of cars in car parks, used to evoke visions of lovely girls. Now those odours evoke only a funny sort of nostalgia for all that frenzy, because now I can be cool. Now I can go to a dance with the score on the board.

It was strange that I no longer carried all that anxiety I used to have with girls. For so many months, years, I had thought I would never get to actually kiss a girl on the lips, let alone fuck with one. My only experience of kissing had been the powdered cheeks of my old aunts. So it was with some feeling of triumph that I left the guest house with Gillian. We were laughing as we negotiated the small track through the bush gums to the wide gravel road that passed the hall. The music was already in the air, awakening old anxieties. I had listened to the sound of dancing for so long without participating that my nerve was now seriously in doubt. 'Be cool!' I told myself. 'Check your responses!' Not to respond could be tough, but then you had to respond to ridicule, and quickly.

The senior blokes in the club were suavely squiring their hot numbers into the hall. Impressive. 'Hey!' I told myself, 'I'm doing the same thing!' I lowered my shoulders, slitted my eyes. Gillian looked incredible in a white dress with a lacy bodice, and high heels brought her to within two inches of my height. She walked with a sort of cat-strut, absolutely confident. When we entered the hall we were immediately the focus of attention. I thought, 'shit they reckon I shouldn't be here because I pulled out of the crew.' I pulled myself up defensively, but the president of the club, Ron Thorne, nodded at me and smiled. Even when we had won the state championships he hadn't looked at me.

'How's it going?' he asked.

'Not bad thanks mate,' I said, tough and tight and then feeling for an instant like a real phoney. As I introduced Gillian, I thought, 'why should I feel like a phoney?'

'Pleased to meet you,' Ron said, smiling, and the girl on his arm beamed. Other blokes were nodding at me, and we moved through into the hall on the wave of goodwill that was sweeping in our direction.

The music was not traditional jazz so it was easy to jive to. As I took the first step to the music, I realised why I was suddenly so popular. My appearance in the sand dunes when Rachel was being molested had given me celebrity status. People had obviously been talking about me and had made me out to be something other than I was. I was under no illusions about my scene in the dunes. I knew I had fumbled it all the way, I'd performed no great acts.

And right now my dancing wasn't much better. For three years I had been preparing for this, dancing to waltz and fox-trot tunes at boarding school with a male friend as partner. The lesson had been conducted by a professional dancing master and his sexy wife, but she had been there merely for demonstration and none of us had got to dance with her, although she was languidly stripped as the dancers lay in their beds every Thursday night, dance night. Meanwhile, we had practised dancing and jiving in the dormitories most weekends during unsupervised periods. But it hadn't been the real thing. Now, as Gillian started easily into twists and turns and I found her balance through her hands, my awareness of how to move improved by three hundred percent in the first dance. As my confidence increased through her, so did the energy of her turns, her white dress swirling to reveal long competent legs. It struck me then that she was one of those girls I had admired through dance hall windows for the past two years, the ones who had inspired in me the depths of envy when I had seen absolute morons dancing with such marvellous creatures. And now here I was pushing her with a casual wrist into perfect pirouettes — the master! It's always amazed me that, on one level, I could not be deluded in any way, and yet on another level I was the biggest mug of them all. So tonight was no exception.

My old mates from the surf boat crowded around between dances and began to mock me, carrying on as if I really was a close mate whose every weakness they knew.

'I reckon you're still the same slow bastard!' George began the jibes. It's incredible how friends can't stand a change in your status. Even if you've done something good they can't stand it.

'Yeah, he was always asleep in the boat,' Jack said. 'I bet you just fell over that bastard!'

'No.' I said. 'It was a bit better than that.'

'Yeah?'

'Yeah! So why don't you piss off?'

'Tough eh!' George said.

'Tougher than you'll ever know,' I said. I hardly knew what the words meant when I uttered them but I knew I was prepared to back them up. My anger was building fast. Then Gillian touched my arm and the rage dissolved. I grinned at her and we began to dance. Acting on momentary impulse, I put my hand over George's face and with an open palm screwed it around. I smiled at him from the heat of my jiving movements. 'Remember?' I said, wanting him to know that last year I had beaten him when we fought in the dunes.

'Remember what, shit head?' he said loud over the music.

'You've got a poor memory.'

We left the dance early because I wanted to get my hands between Gillian's legs. I suggested it when she returned from the Powder Room with her lips a shining carmine. She wasn't too pleased though, because most people were looking at her as she danced and that sort of admiration must be hard to toss aside. But I pressed her anyway. 'You're looking gorgeous,' I said. 'I really want to make love to you. I want to kiss your breasts and stroke your legs.' I pressed myself against her with a faint bulge that could harden instantly. These last few days all shyness had left me. I was blundering around in a man's image, and no matter how awkward the fit, I was tasting some freedom.

Halfway along the track I kissed her lips gently. Finding her legs close together I said: 'Widen your legs.' She obeyed and I stroked her shiny pants, 'I can feel you're really wet,' I said. 'I want to fuck you properly.'

She drew back a little. 'No,' she said, but she stroked me. 'You can put it there,' she said. I put it between her legs. 'No,' she said. 'Wait. Come into the bushes.' She turned her back to me. 'Undo me.' I undid her dress and her bra and she turned to me with her breasts bare and inviting, and they were so soft when I kissed into them. I could feel the smoothness of her thighs trembling. When I came I was driving against an elegantly swaying woman. It was too much. I began groaning with the pleasure and the pain. 'Ssssssh,' she said. 'We don't want anyone to hear.' I was past caring and that didn't impress her too much. She kissed me, laughing to stifle the groans. 'You're really noisy!' she said. We were giggling breathlessly when we stumbled back onto the track.

'Now we should go walking on the beach,' I said. 'But I don't think it would be a wise move.'

'No,' she said. 'Definitely not.'

Back in my room, after Gillian had changed, we lay on the bed talking. 'Something should be done about the bastard,' I said.

'I can't see there is much to do,' she offered.

'It seems that some people can get away with these things because other people don't really care.'

'Rachel says it seems as if the bastards get away with it all the time, but she says everybody is always given what they deserve. She told me about a Jewess, a dancer, who was about to be processed into a gas chamber, and one of the Nazi guards recognised her as a dancer, and told her to dance. So she did. But she danced close to the officer, so close that he was disoriented and distracted, and she grabbed his pistol and shot him. They beat her to death, but Rachel said when she saw the woman dancing and then shooting, it was as if the woman recognised that this was the high point of her life; this moment of protest and violence was the thing she had been born to do.'

'Jesus,' I said, 'how come Rachel is telling you these things?'

'I don't know. She was talking about women and the strong things they could do. She said just because men make playthings of women, it doesn't mean that women have to accept that. She told me not to let men *use* me, in the sense that one can enjoy sex so much that you attach yourself to men for no other reason than the pleasure.'

'Sounds a good idea to me!'

'Rubbish!' she said, and she grabbed a pillow and whacked it down hard on my head. 'I think she's right about that. It was a terrific relief for me to hear somebody talking like that.'

'Is that why you've been on about the "many men" thing?'

'Probably.'

'Are you just calculating on the pleasure? Or do you feel there would be safety in numbers — that you wouldn't get so attached to one person?'

'I don't know what I feel, yet.'

'Well,' I said, being the ham. 'If I can be of any help!' But beneath the banter I was really thinking about Rachel's story of the dancer and the brute — that dancer had been really something. She had simply taken control of the situation and ordered her own death on her own terms. It was remarkable. I wondered if I would ever be in a similar situation and be able to reject the impulse to crawl for mercy.

## CHAPTER 7

Rachel became the focus of my curiosity. She was a medium through which Gillian was learning more about the nature of human beings. And I was learning by association. Whenever I passed her during the day I greeted her effusively.

At first I was bewildered by these spontaneous greetings of mine, but then I recognised that they were intended to encourage Rachel to accept me. I looked forward to learning more. And I wanted to tell her more. I was desperate to understand myself and I hoped that by getting acquainted with other extremes of experience, I could begin to locate the sense in my own behaviour.

Rachel was a tall woman who was close to being angular. She was handsome: clear-faced with a straight gaze. Her cheek bones were high and her mouth wide. Her hair was in one straight and careless plait that might have been created quickly by a woman about to play a game of tennis. She wore plain colours, but her dresses were cut in a simple style that gave her movements an easy flair. In bathing togs she was shapely but her flesh wobbled slightly, as though she had fattened a little rapidly to that shape rather than arrived at it gradually. She did eat voraciously, and if she drank too quickly she would sometimes laugh in a high-pitched screech that had nothing to do with humour. Sometimes it would get out of control and she and Hans would have to leave the room where my parents or their friends were hosting pre-dinner drinks. Down the corridor you could hear the screech become sobbing. Apparently it had nothing to do with how she was feeling. Instead it was some physically imposed condition that Rachel often cursed. On one occasion she actually laughed about it. For me it was further proof that she was the fount of all suffering. I had read Dumas' *The Man in the Iron Mask*, the story of the man whose extraordinary laughter, the result of an early operation to make him a carnival act, had erupted while he was speaking in Parliament, attempting to improve the conditions of the poor. In his emotional state, a blast of laughter had reverberated from behind his iron mask, and the members who had begun to be affected by his plea for justice, felt they had been the butt of clever satire. I fantasised that Rachel was afflicted in a similarly disturbing way and so could only pass on her knowledge in private situations.

I indulged in more speculation about her relationship with Hans. Had they come together because of a mutual understanding of the depths of suffering? Had they been hurt in the same way? Or did Rachel have a victim of her own? Perhaps guilt had placed Hans within her reach. And did she, knowing the depths of his guilt, only feel safe with a person who was totally committed to redemption? Or did she use him in a way that would slowly destroy him? I had no answers. Hans comforted Rachel at all times. He hovered, served and explained her idiosyncracies. He told the story of her scarred leg: of how because of her youth, fellow marchers had helped her to survive, and that she had survived despite her wounded and poisoned legs. These were all marvellous things to me. They smacked of true heroism and grand gestures. While the Australian war memorials were full of the grand gestures under fire, and it was the fighting spirit that was always glorified. The misery of it all was rarely on display in those war memorials.

For all my ideas, and a distinct willingness to talk, I could tell Rachel didn't even consider me. The judge was the person she did confront seriously, and this time she wasn't betrayed by her laughter. It was one evening at pre-dinner drinks in my parents' room, after another marvellous day of sun and surf. Their guests were pleasantly tired and had dropped the barriers that normally prevented any significant conversation. The judge launched into a discussion about the aboriginal middens he had seen during his walks along various parts of the coast.

'... and there are oven sites where they buried their dead.'

Newspapers and magazines often carried stories about the gas chambers and ovens where millions of Jews had perished, and where all trace of their existence had been obliterated. But I was still dismayed to hear the word 'ovens' in Rachel's presence. I looked away from her, attempting, I suppose, to avoid any guilt by association with the comment. But my embarrassment was just as much of an affectation as my innocence was.

My father made a valiant attempt to camouflage the comment. 'Personally,' he said, 'I think such walks should only be taken after a heavy meal . . . a sort of punishment, to rid one of that dazed feeling.'

It wasn't much of an offering, but it began a desultory conversation on good food requiring good surroundings. Then there was a loud contemptuous laugh from Rachel. I decided it had been prompted by the innocent conversations of those who had never been deprived. Did she find these people comical after surviving that incandescent evil of man? I hoped so.

Rachel walked across to the window. 'That was a bit rough,' my father said quietly to the judge. 'Nonsense,' the judge said loudly. 'There is no association. The ovens of aboriginal people have nothing in common with civilized people.' His words were pitched for the room to hear.

'Exactly!' Rachel said pouncing on him. 'Civilized people have shown themselves able to live in more filth and cruelty than any primitive people.'

'Not true,' the judge declared categorically. 'Can you imagine those middens when they were in use? Nothing more than stinking mounds of discarded food. Interesting phenomena now, but flies then would have made it a stinking rubbish tip.'

'And how do mounds of human bones make it better for civilization?'

I knew my laugh was strident, but also supportive. I left the room after that, exalted by these struggles from the cutting edge of life, but unable to disguise my own restlessness and frustrated desires to participate.

I began my introspection again, and I came to the conclusion that I was nothing more than a callow youth wanting to use ideas for ego stimulation. Was this visible? Of course. Everything was visible to her. Despite my open greetings, hers were never more than perfunctory. I began to be jealous of her talks with Gillian, while still respecting their ease of conversation.

Their discussions were animated and I could not approach them during those times. Strangely, no one else at the guest house did either. It was as if the two women had such an obvious affinity that others knew instinctively not to intrude. They would talk over coffee, standing only a short distance away from the others, but as if isolated in some charmed circle: Gillian tall with a defiant and fresh beauty, and Rachel, about the same height, but laughing and talking openly and familiarly. They seemed like very old friends. Hans would watch them with a smile, glancing up occasionally from a conversation to see Rachel talking there with Gillian, and he would be reassured.

'She's a good friend, isn't she?' I asked Gillian one night after we had all finished coffee.

'She's terrific.'

'What do you find to talk about?'

She laughed at me, looking directly into my eyes with a teasing smile. 'We talk about everything.'

'Mostly sex then.'

'Not at all. Would you like me to tell you *everything* we talk about?'

'Probably,' I laughed, caught out.

'It's not that interesting. We just get along well.'

'Does she talk about her experiences?'

'Not that much. I try to avoid it, because she sort of gets locked into explanations. She talks very rapidly then, and assumes that I know more than I do, and if I query her she gets impatient and dismissive, but it doesn't stop her telling me.'

'As if she's obsessed by it?'

'Yes, as though she's been down that path before and there is something she has to repeat continually, I mean she's right . . . it sounds right, but that doesn't matter. It's saying it again, and again, with the same emphasis that seems to be important. It also makes me sorry for her, because whatever it is behind the story, she's never going to get over it.'

'You mean she's not telling you the real story.'

'I don't want to hear it.'

'Aaah, so you're the chosen one. She'd tell you if you would let her. Is that it?'

'I don't know, really. I suppose I do stop her. I change the subject wildly. It's as if it's her story, and I don't want it to affect me.'

'You think it could?'

'Come on, I don't know what it is.'

'Well *you* said it.'

'P'raps I don't want to know too much. I mean she knows stuff that's probably ruined her life.'

'And it could ruin yours?'

'Hey, I don't know.'

'Why don't you take a fly?'

'A what?'

'A chance.'

'I've taken plenty of those, only a few of them any good.'

'Well she might need to talk about it with somebody. Why not you?'

'We'll see,' she said.

The lights of the holiday town were carpeted across the foothills of the ranges and it was good to be watching them like this with Gillian. Everything was comfortable and safe. The lights of the houses made it seem that all was right in the kitchens and dining-rooms everywhere. Life was progressing everywhere. Despite our fears, civilization was never far away.

## CHAPTER 8

I woke early the next morning before the dawn had lined the blind with light. It was already astonishingly hot. I searched the sheets for coolness and each time my legs or arms found a spot I'd relax back into sleep. But eventually I had to get up and open the window. The smell of the ocean washed into the room with traces of salt and eucalyptus and rotting seaweed. I thought of going to Gillian's room and waking her for an early morning swim. But then I noticed I had that slight shaking and shivering of the body that a fever produces. I convinced myself that the morning was the same for everybody else, so there'd be no point in drawing attention to myself. I turned on the light and it gleamed in the sheen of sweat across my chest. I had no nausea, I felt alright, so where did my body heat come from? Within moments though the ocean breeze cooled me and I pulled the sheet back and slept.

Gillian woke me with a knock on the door. 'Aren't you going for breakfast?' I felt terrible. I struggled to compose my slack face with usual expressions but nothing seemed to fit. 'What's wrong?' she asked.

'Just death warmed up,' I said.

'I'll get your mother.'

That set me back a bit. 'Hell no,' I said. 'I just didn't sleep.' She sat beside me on the bed and rumpled my hair. 'Do you want breakfast in bed?'

'That's something my mother would prescribe.'
'Sometimes it helps.'
'I'll go for a swim.'
'Well I won't wait,' she said. 'I'm famished.' She rose from the bed and left the room.

This morning she was wearing a cotton dress with deep green and purple bands. It looked marvellous above her tanned legs. My head cleared slightly like a ratchet clicking. At least something moved there. I got out of bed without too much effort.

The morning had a peculiar light and a burnt copper feel about it. It wasn't until I was high up the main dune that I realised there was a strong northerly blowing. Without thinking my mind supplied a comment: this is the day.

It wasn't unusual for intuitions like that to occur to me. It was the reason why masters continually reported to my parents that I wasn't living up to expectations. My mind was on another tangent, that was all. I followed through the most obscure ideas of my own creations, often abstracting myself from my surroundings as I explored and marked boundaries in my mind. So naturally when I was working with material I had already explored, masters tended to think me capable of more advanced work. Not at all. It was simply that I rejected anything I didn't learn or discover myself, whether in extra curricula books or my own imaginings. I never returned to conventional learning because people out to give me lectures never taught me anything.

I continued up the dune and at the top I resisted looking anywhere but at the ocean. It was slapping massively at the sand line. Waves of green and molten glass were sliding in their thin crests whipped by the wind and turned back in arcs of white before breaking. It reminded me of the cow-lick hair styles my friends and I used to design when I was seven years old at state school. That had been a comfortable time. Nobody had expected anything of me. In those days I loved roaming the streets and parks, yabbying in ornamental ponds and playing in my friends' backyards. My parents hadn't pushed me then. I had no idea whether the pushing had been good or bad, but I suspected that when they sent me to boarding school they lost me.

I strode into the ocean without looking to the north. Maybe school had been a good thing after all. I had escaped my father's obsessions, although I never knew exactly what they were. But I did know when I had come into conflict with them, because his heavy jaw would begin to tick, and if I had been really bad, he would begin a tight whistle. Somehow I gathered my own obsessions from further back. I remember thinking that perhaps memories could be passed down. How else could I explain the nameless fears and certainties that came to me occasionally?

It suddenly seemed strange to be able to retain thoughts as I dived into the water, and to continue them as I swam. I had developed the habit of monitoring my swimming style. But today, for the first time, I didn't, I swam without knowing how I swam. My thoughts continued: it was time now to make all my own decisions, to expect nothing of my parents. They would no longer be of any help. Their support now would only be a gift of all their prejudices and poor decisions. I had to make my own mistakes. I had known all that before, but now I was totally convinced of it.

I turned off my introspection and dived for the bottom. I held onto the sand with my hands and stayed there for a minute looking up at the waves moving across the surface: a fish-eye view. How many billions of fish had looked at the surface like that for how many millions of years before one of the bastards had a revelation that pushed between its deepest reflexes, and it shoved its head from the waves to look at what else was around.

When I pushed to the surface to look at the northern

sky a wave smashed from behind. The water hit the back of my throat and I suppressed a coughing fit. I sucked for air and when my senses cleared I looked at the sky. At first I wasn't sure if the haze was simply atomised spray from the huge breaking waves. But the greenish tinge was alien. I dried myself as I watched the sky. It was becoming darker. I wrapped the towel around my neck and sprinted up the dune. Over the ranges there was black curling smoke. I took off for the guest house with bounding strides. A few quick steps across the rough bitumen and I was in the gate and up the stairs to the verandah.

The judge was at the door, sipping his coffee as he listened to his wife. 'It's a fire!' I yelled to everyone. The judge turned to me with a 'not-you-again' look on his face, but his glance caught the moving plateau of smoke and as the shock registered, his mouthful of coffee splattered over his wife. She looked at him without comprehension.

'We're in trouble,' I called to my father. 'It's a big one with a northerly behind it!''

I was pleased to be able to sound knowledgeable. Well I am anyway, I confirmed to myself.

My father threaded his way through the group. Seeing the direction of the fire and noting the rising wind he said, 'It's already cut the road. I think we'll all be fighting this one.' The judge moved to the door behind me and I realised that he hoped a closer uninterrupted look would reveal the scene to be less frightful. In fact it was worse than we could see. He looked seaward, searching the sky as if he was sure that his friends at Government level had not forgotten him and that a plane would soon be flying in to remove him from this predicament. He'd shown me that most men strive for prestigious positions because they sure as hell don't want to be forgotten when the bad times come. Natural enough, but sickening to see. I hoped I would remember that lesson, especially in a crisis.

At the moment I was exhilarated by the fire, so I had

no immediate problems in maintaining a bold demeanour. Other guests had crowded out onto the stairs, so the judge had to move down, a step at a time. Clearly he didn't like leaving his commanding position, but he'd have to get into the action if he wanted to maintain that position in these circumstances. The prestige alone no longer counted. But I stopped myself from indulging in the spectacle of the judge's dithering. It would be childish of me to want the man's downfall while doing nothing myself to solve the problem at hand.

The truck that usually pulled the surfboat thundered past the guest house, but on seeing the crowd of potential fire-fighters it stopped with a squeal of brakes and billows of dust, then it reversed back to the gate. Ron Thorne leapt out and yelled, 'Have we got any takers?' The judge started to move back up the stairs onto the verandah. Ron stood there in amazement as he saw his potential fire-fighters disappearing. My father and I walked down to meet him.

'What have you got to fight with?' my father asked.

'Well we've got these bags on the back and we're just going to water them at the pump.'

'You'll need more than that for this fire. The bastard'll be uncontrollable in this wind, specially in the timber country. Can you get tanks and pumps? That's the least you'll need just to survive.'

'Shit!' Ron said. In most of the other emergencies he'd dealt with there was too much water.

'Those dairy farmers will have pumps,' my father said. 'You'd better get something.' He backed away. Advice was all my old man was going to give. 'I'll organise something in the town,' my father said retreating. 'Stupid bastard,' he muttered as we returned to the guest house. That was strange, because I'd often heard Ron calling innocent swimmers stupid bastards.

'It'll take a while to get here,' my father said. 'When

it drops into those gullies up there it'll be out of the wind. It takes a while to burn up to wind level again. Although if the wind picks up stronger we could be Christmas.'

'Hey!' he yelled up to the figures on the verandah, 'We're going to need a few people if the fire gets down here, and it looks as though it will.'

'You know who started this don't you? It's that farmer. He wants to burn the bloody town,' I hissed at my father.

'Well it looks like he's probably done it this time.'

'What are you going to do about him?'

'Fucking nothing,' he said dropping into his farmer's language, which he usually left behind when he came down to the sea.

'But he'll just start more. Christ can't you see that?'

'He's not our business.'

'Shit he isn't.' I could scarcely contain my fury.

He whirled on me. 'Stay out of this! You have no idea of how serious this can get.'

'I do. I know the score.'

'Well just keep out of the areas where he might be.' He looked at the few men who were coming down the stairs and then turned to me, 'Know the score, Christ!' he said with contempt.

'Stuff you!' I answered.

'Don't be silly about this,' he added quickly as the men came across the lawn to meet him. 'If you blunder off there's no way you can be of any use. Right now you can help us here.'

I looked at him as he turned to the men. 'Blunder', I thought. So that's how he sees me. All the time I thought I was getting myself together, he was thinking, 'blunderer'. The bastard had been patronising me, not telling me how he felt, not having it out in the open, hiding his feelings and ideas because it was easier for him to have little regard for me. Not only that but he was obviously avoiding any confrontation or challenge; he had been for years, because he was comfortable with the thought that his son was a blunderer. Fuck him! If he wasn't careful he would have me challenging him all the way. No, that was bullshit. The best thing would be to leave the place. Already I had decided to leave his sphere of influence and avoid the habit of dropping back into it. I know you, you bastard. I found I was humming with my rage, a consistent determined hum.

I moved with the group of men to the workshop behind the house, and as my father handed out the shovels, the crosscut saw, and anything at all that could be used to clear ground, I was very close to taking a shovel and whacking him across the head. He would never know how close. Fuck his superiority act. I leaned the shovel that was handed to me up against the wall and headed off. I told Gillian that I was going to see what I could do up where they would be filling trucks at the town's water terminal. She looked at me and grinned. 'You've had a run-in with your father haven't you?'

'Sure have, the bastard.'

'What's he want you to do?'

'*Stop blundering around* was how he put it.'

'Did he?' she said. 'What did he mean by that?'

'That I was a nuisance to him I suppose. Fuck him!' My anger was about to overwhelm me. I was close to lighting my own fires. I turned to go, obsessed by my own violent passions.

'Hey!' Gillian called, 'Remember me?'

I turned back and hugged her. 'I'm really sorry. There's no excuse for that.'

'That's alright,' she said. 'I think you're frightened.'

More than that, I was high on savagery and images of triumphant revenges. I had no way of linking that with fear, although I knew something had created the rage. I had thought it had been a fusing of my outrage at the farmer's abuses of Gillian and Rachel, and now the fire behind the pall of smoke twisting wildly above the ranges at the back of the town. But I knew already that the idea of the fire appealed to me: it gave me something to do, somewhere to direct my uneasiness. I kissed into Gillian's neck. The skin and her soft hair were comforting. It was exhilarating knowing that she accepted me. She ran her hand across my cheek and I smiled at her with an expression that was now connecting itself with my real feelings. Previously, I had adopted expressions that I had seen on my parents and their friends, assuming that by doing so I was somehow becoming an adult.

'You've never smiled like that before,' she said.

'How do you mean?' I asked, hoping that everyone was not as perceptive as she was. But I'd only ever been myself when I was with her.

'I've never seen all your teeth,' she said laughing.

'Stuff my teeth!' I said. 'What about the rest of me?' I ran my hand across the back of her legs as I walked away. 'I've got to do something today,' I said. 'At least find out what's going on.'

'Don't think you've got to do *too* much,' she called after me. 'Everyone can just walk into the sea if it gets too bad. There's no need for any heroes just to save other people's houses.'

My fingers still felt her ready acceptance of my touch, and at the gate I held my hand up in a quick parting gesture. I jogged slowly down to the park where a gravel road ran close to the river, the only place where trucks could take water.

There was a motley collection of farm vehicles already there: some old trucks used for hay-carting and market days, now carrying water tanks, a couple of tractors with tanks on trailers, and one truck from the Country Fire

Authority. Hoses snaked down from them into the water. The heat from their pumps distorted the air like a mirage, and it was as if a gust of cool wind would carry them all away.

'How bad is it?' I asked a group leaning on the fenders of the CFA truck, while a mate watched the rising level of water in the tank on the tray.

'You want to lend a hand do you? You reckon you're up to it?'

'I've fought fires before. Every bloody summer I can remember,' I said.

'Shit, we need you then mate,' a tall lean bloke said. He was dressed in old army clothes and had a fag dribbling from his mouth. He was having a lend of me. 'We don't get too many experienced hands down this way. Rarely get fires. You reckon you can tell us how to do it then?'

'I can help,' I said laughing.

'Well you mightn't need to save the town,' he mocked, only a small twitch of his fag giving a clue to his humour. 'We've got a wind change see. It's already hit the old town up the way. But we might need some help though. Even if it blows back on itself we'll have to put out the small fires.'

His mates had nothing to contribute to the conversation. They were watching him with appreciation. The bloke watching the water level sniggered once, and the two beefy blokes either side of him were grinning.

'How did it start?' I asked.

'How do they usually start?' the laconic one rejoined.

'Someone playing with matches,' I said bluntly.

'It's usually lightning down this way, mate.'

'Yeah,' said the bloke on the tray, 'and down here bloody young squirts watch who they're talking to, hey.'

The laconic one squinted up to his mate. 'C'mon Charlie he knows what he's talking about.'

'So fuckin' what.' Charlie replied.

'So we could do with a hand.'

'Yeah,' Charlie said. 'Well he's the bastard going with the sheila from the cafe, right.'

The laconic one pushed off from the truck fender. 'Bit of alright with the sheilas, are you?'

'He's full of bullshit,' I said, surprised that I felt more at home talking to these blokes than I did with my parents.

Before going away to school I only mixed with the blokes around the property, the shearing sheds and the railway siding. They had been most of my companionship until I was ten years old.

I walked away when some other farmers came up to discuss which roads they would negotiate to get into the back country. From the way they talked there was apparently a criss-cross of tracks that had been grown over or forgotten and only the laconic one knew where they were. As I passed the old boat sheds on the river, gusts of wind from the ranges dumped ash in my hair. I could tell that the smoke had shifted direction; it had now been moulded parallel to the ranges, almost a reflection of the fire in the sky, and there was a redness in the smoke that terrified me. I wet my finger and held it high, but the air was turbulent where it rushed between the boat shed and the high hedges on the other side of the road. I couldn't really be certain of anything.

Further along the bank I saw the round shapes of caravans moving through the trees, and the odd tent was coming down. People were preparing for flight. I wondered where they were headed. It would have to be the showgrounds where the summer grass had shrunk to nothing after some cattle had been run there to clean up, or the beach, the safest place.

By the time I had reached the guest house the change was even more apparent. A fresh ocean wind had blown the air clean, and even the sooty tinge had gone from the light; the cloud of smoke was moving away to the north. Several caravans lumbered into the car park close to the beach and the drivers left their cars to gaze at the sky.

## CHAPTER 9

After the sunset the night became a scene from a magnificent hell. Deep oranges and greens lit the sky. The cliffs to the west showed their best red light and our legs, as we waded through the shallows, were bathed in gold and orange. It was a liberating experience. A world that could be changed by colours was a novel thing. It could renew the spirit. We didn't think of the destruction of the hills, or of the danger; although I did think of the mad artist lurking up there. His actions had changed this part of the world. Tonight it might only be the colours, tomorrow a black swathe would be cut through the ranges, and if this display didn't satisfy him he would undoubtedly attempt to rearrange the mathematics of the human life in the town. Watching the colours on Gillian's legs I could understand for a moment how people lived with war. Beyond the fear, it gave extra dimensions to life. This night, containing the colours and some of the dangers of war, gave an added licence to behaviour. When I caught up with Gillian I knew she felt it too. Her self-assurance was exhilarating.

'We can swim just beyond the point,' she suggested, taking my hand and tugging me into a run.

My pleasure was that I could be myself with her and not be judged, or at least not care if I was judged. I was prepared to be honest with her; moreover I felt I could only be that way. This is me, I thought when I kissed her, and I love you.

'I love you,' I said aloud.

'Darling,' she said very softly. 'I love you.'

I undid her shorts and let them drop to the ground. She stepped neatly out of them. I opened her shirt and looked at her. She grinned.

'Satisfied?' she asked.

'Beautiful!' I said. She threw off her shirt, pulled down her pants and looked at me.

'I hope you're coming in too.'

'I like the great colours,' I said.

She was traced with orange and a flickering red. The water beyond her was a molten metal shushing close to her feet. Her body was slim, but her hips curved outrageously. It was as if I was viewing a secret delight. I stripped off my clothes and tossed them over my shoulder randomly. I didn't care if I lost them. She took her pants on one toe and flicked them close to her shorts.

We walked to the water a few feet apart. I would have hated the cliche' of walking to the sea holding hands! This was a wild night. When I hit the water my shoulder seemed to split with pain, but within moments it had accustomed itself to the salt water.

'Hey!' I called when I emerged from a dive and saw her still heading out, water tucking neatly around her hips.

'Not too far!' I didn't want a big fish devouring her first. Night swimming has its eerie moments. A cruising shark could have been drawn by the unusual colours dappling its befuddled short-sighted eyes. Perhaps similar lights from burning ships had attracted it before. We needed the possibility of getting back to the beach. From where I had stopped a big shark would ground itself five steps in. The water was warm where I lay. Gillian turned to face me.

'Come on out here,' she called. The image of gliding sharks no longer bothered me. A stride before I reached her she dived neatly away. I didn't grab, sensing a slow ballet. But she surfaced beside me. Her lips were slippery when I kissed her and she moved them over my face, licking my ears and breathing there with hot breath. She turned in my arms like an acrobat. She was stroking herself against my body, enjoying every nuance of movement. When I finally stopped her I was weak with pleasure. Entering her from the coolness of the water I felt her cunt intensely hot.

'Don't bloody move!' I whispered slowly through closed teeth, and I held her tight there as she laughed and tried to wriggle her hips energetically.

'Jesus don't!' I said, but began laughing and coming simultaneously. I had to check my convulsions for fear of drowning her. My orgasm seemed to catch two moments there, and her small moans became squeals as she launched into lustful thrustings.

'Not so bad,' she laughed as she pushed away from me.

I could have slept then, confident that water would keep us suspended. I wondered about the trail of semen, and imagined the substance suspended like glue in the ocean, a fish food delicacy to be rolled in the gullet in the same way a connoisseur relished a wine. I imagined the fish swarming in the water: 'Hey, it's some sort of night humans' come in the warm water. They descend from the land to the sea and rock against each other. It is one of the amazing stories of human behaviour. No fish knows why they do it. Even the great fish eccentrics, the big salmon, are at a loss to reason their behaviour. Are they planning to build a human being with gills?'

The cliffs above the rocks were no longer red, but had absorbed tone from the sky. The orange glow was around us in the water as we walked. The colour was too sensational to be enjoyed without wondering whether it wasn't all some sort of artifice.

'I wish I could say something about this without being corny,' Gillian said.

I wasn't sure whether she was talking of the event or of the colourful night. Moments later the wind ceased and the water beyond the breakers mirrored an oily darkness gleaming with orange licks. The thin skin that finally rushed over the sand to our feet was part of the living night.

'It's fantastic,' Gillian said. 'How many people have walked in nights like this?' I breathed deeply and caught a tinge of smoke.

'The country nights are best,' Gillian added, and I recalled irrigation flats with their sudden cool waves of air on scorching nights: frogs generating darkness with pulsing sounds, the damp smells of a living and dying earth washing the senses, and the sky heavy with sparklers. We negotiated the rocks, illuminated by the weird glow. Looking back I saw our footprints dissolving behind us in the soaking sand.

'Are we part of something?' Gillian asked, looking from the sky to me. 'Just suppose we were part of something, what would it be?'

'The wind's changed direction,' I said. 'By the morning we might be part of a bonfire.'

'Seriously?' she said, and I found I wasn't too concerned by the danger of the fire.

'I don't know,' I said, 'but we would have to be part of some object's thought processes. If we think something we pass it onto others, just the way a brain works.'

As we reached the dunes opposite the guest house, the smoke was thick. From the top of the dunes we could see the ranges profiled by a reddish glow that appeared and disappeared as the smoke waved in the wind like a grotesque scarf.

'What happens now?' Gillian asked as we watched the sky.

'It'll be burning back on ground that's already been covered. It'll give them areas to work out of. I don't know the country though.'

## CHAPTER 10

My father shook me awake in the early morning. It took me moments to understand where I was. I rose from the bed, incapable of listening to him, and staggered to the window. I didn't trust his judgement any longer. I hadn't realised it until I asked myself why I was moving to check the situation and my father was standing there waiting to tell me. Smoke blurred the hedge, and the tennis court was no longer visible. The hedge was rocking in the smoky wind and the sound of it should have woken me earlier. The old guest house was creaking.

'They need everyone,' my father said.

'A fire like this can't be stopped.'

'The wind is changing constantly,' he continued.

'I'm not going into the ranges,' I said. 'You'd have to be bloody stupid.' For some reason I thought he was expecting me to be in the front line. Fuck that.

'No one can fight this wind. They're working the edges of it, keeping it straight to the sea.'

'How far away is it?' I sat down on the bed and rubbed my eyes, which seemed to enrage him.

'Jesus Christ!' he threw at me.

'Listen I'm cool,' I said, and for the first time I knew what I meant.

'You're *cool*,' he hissed. 'What sort of rubbish is that?' He turned around to leave.

'It might be rubbish to you,' I said, 'but that's exactly what I am. How far away is the fire?'

He glared at me from the doorway. 'It could be half an hour, it could be a day.'

'I'm going for a swim,' I said.

'What do you mean a swim?' he shouted.

'You went on with your life when I warned you,' I said. 'Do you really expect me to jump around like some jiggling puppet at one word from you, Christ!'

I stepped out of my pyjama shorts and pulled on damp bathers. My father walked away up the passage.

The heat hit me the instant I stepped from the door. The smoke was black and laying down cinders like snow flakes. I'd once stood on the mountain behind Hobart in a snow storm. Although it had been coming out of a black sky the mood had been gentle. This was violent and hot. I turned back to warn Gillian. Her door was open and she was curled so comfortably you could have imagined a girl who had never been insecure in her life. I touched her shoulder gently.

'Hey!' I said, 'Wake up.'

I sat on the bed and stroked her cheek as she opened her eyes. Those slanted green eyes. They stared at me momentarily without recognition and then she grinned.

'Listen to the wind,' I said. 'We seem to be in some trouble. The fire's broken out again and looks like coming down on the town.'

'Are we in any real danger here?'

'Didn't you say we could always run into the sea? Well I'm going down there now.'

'You mean do I want a swim or something?'

'Or something.'

She pushed back the sheet and kicked me off the bed. 'Swim only,' she laughed.

She pulled up the blind and was instantly still. 'God,' she said in a small voice. 'What does this mean?'

'It means there's a big fire in the hills. It doesn't necessarily mean it's going to get here, although my personal opinion is that it will.'

'It looks like it's here now.'

'I think the main fire is about ten miles away and as it burnt its own firebreak yesterday it'll take a while to get around it. That's if anybody is fighting it.'

'And you're going swimming?'

'Sure. There's plenty of time for me to get involved. It must be a magnificent sight from the ocean. Imagine the sensations: freezing water, hot winds and the smell of burning.' I lay back on the floor laughing, watching her legs.

'Fiddle while Rome burns sort of stuff?' she asked.

'No, my contribution is not going to make much difference and I want to experience it all.'

'You didn't start it by any chance did you?'

And that stopped me for a moment. 'Yeah, I suppose I *am* enjoying it,' I said.

'Why are you like that?' she asked.

'Is it that bad?'

'I don't know. You're the only one who could know that. But it seems to me you might like it all too much.'

'You think that's bad?'

'I don't know. I don't know enough. How much do you like being outside everybody else?'

'I think everybody does.'

'I think everybody else would worry about it.'

'I don't enjoy it enough to have started it.'

'But you like it enough to be there at the finish, examining everything, getting some sort of kick out of it.'

I tried for the touchstone, that feeling I bounced my emotions off: how do I feel now?

'But,' I said earnestly, 'there is no compulsion to chase it, create it.'

'But would you avoid it?' she said. Hey, I thought, she is very smart. I could see that at this point I didn't have any reverse gear. I couldn't see myself backing off.

'What are you talking about? What could I avoid?'

'You want to trail along hoping that behind it all there'll be that bloody maniac.'

'I don't hope that, I just don't think I'd walk away from it.'

'It's the same thing,' she said. I sat against the wall and looked at her. She was sitting against the dressing table, her legs crossed. She had no thought of how vulnerable she looked. The baby doll pyjamas she wore had lace around the legs. But her attitude was as if she were wearing a three-piece suit. It seemed that the best girls were those who melted in bed but were tough as hell when they were on their feet.

'What would you like me to do? *Is* there anything that I can do? We're all here now. It's not as if any of us is going anywhere.'

The smoke was entering the guest house — the smell of it, not the substance.

'What are any of us going to do?'

She looked in the mirror and picked up a brush from the dresser. Staring quizzically at herself she began to brush her hair. I looked out the window and watched as the men of the guest house continued with the jobs they had started yesterday. Branches that shook too close to the house were being taken off. My father had a saw and was attacking a huge branch of a fig tree close to the weatherboard bungalows. The Squadron Leader was yelling but his voice was lost in the high wind. The judge wasn't about. The fire would have to wipe out most of the town to get to the guest house, so nobody was being optimistic.

Gillian had quickly plaited her long hair and curled it about her head — no stray flame was going to set her alight.

'You're not swimming?' she said as she turned.

She was angry and for the first time in my life I began to talk about my parents.

'I'm not going to be ordered about by my old man any more,' I said. 'The bastard thinks I'm some sort of slave whose future he should have a hand in every step of the way. He thinks he will give out the freedoms when the appropriate times come.'

'And you'd die rather than obey him?' she asked. 'And I'm not being facetious. Today seems pretty desperate.'

'It's not as bad as it looks unless you want to save other people's property, right.'

She held my hand. 'Are you sure?'

'Yes.'

'You wouldn't have me on?'

'Well, only sometimes.' I kissed her, the firmness, the smoothness, a delight. I leaned back and snibbed the door.

'Now?' she asked.

'The closeness of danger,' I said in my hammy actor's voice, 'has always added spice to love-making.'

'Rachel said they used to kill people when they were making love, sometimes the man, sometimes the woman. She said they killed a man they ordered to make love to her.'

'Christ,' I said and stood away from her and the bed.

'Is that where it all ends?' she asked.

All I could think of was that when you try to remove a way of acting and thinking from your character and you look back and see the scar tissue that forms after the removal, you congratulate yourself: yes, it's gone, and reassured you look away. And all the time you are unaware of the developing nerves and blood vessels that are creeping back through the tissues, and then once again you have the spark that reactivates the scar into what it once was. For on hearing of such cruelty I was, for a split second, excited. I crushed it instantly, but I knew it was back, and I knew it was in everyone.

'Is that where the fight begins?' I said. 'If everybody knows they have the capacity for that frightfulness, then they can put a barrier between that and them.'

'Can they?' she asked. 'Really? Aren't most people compulsive?'

'I have no idea,' I said.

I could see she was depressed, as if there were no chance. She was crying.

'But I'm in a position to be happy,' she said. We grabbed at each other for comfort.

'It's the fire,' I said. 'We're loading it all onto some other thing, idea, because we don't want to admit how bloody frightened we are.'

'It can be the other way around,' she said.

'Come down for a swim. These bastards will still be running around trying to organise when we get back.'

'No, you go. I don't like the beach during the day any more.' She smiled at her attempt at humour.

'I'll make it back in five minutes.'

'Take all the time you want, you seem to need to know it all. Everybody else is frightened and you're running around making sure you don't miss out on anything.'

The nature of the beach had changed. It was empty. A rare sight on a summer's day. The breakers were no longer white, but dirty cream from the ash. The sky was dark and racing no more than a hundred metres above the sea. The heat burned my nostrils. On the sand dunes the ti-tree was raging. I imagined the fire sweeping the dunes and saw that with a strong wind the flames would cover anything on the beach. It would be a doubtful refuge for anyone but a strong swimmer.

The water was still cold, although after a dive my skin was covered in wet ash. Beneath the surface I opened my eyes to a clean coolness. It felt good, as though fires and sweaty nights were in the past. I pushed to the surface and rose with the slope of a wave to an exhilarating height. A swift motion as if I was rising into the black sky, and then I was down in the trough watching the wave break away from me to the beach. Christ, I really loved this playing. I felt there wouldn't need to be much in my life except sun and ocean and ... Gillian. I laughed under the water. You didn't have freedom and a beautiful woman as well. A cunningly devised trap was there, one I didn't want to avoid, and I imagined few people would have the strength to do it either.

Out beyond the break line the wind seemed fierce even close to the water and spume from the waves drove back at me with the force of sleet. This was a new sensation and I felt I could continue swimming and join the creatures that played further out. Looking back at the shore line I allowed myself an animal's consciousness, a dolphin's or a killer whale's: the shore line was a scene of destruction, humans murdering each other again, and it was not as if they ate anything they killed; it was only a scene of passing interest unless some of the human leftovers drifted out of the river with the tide. I began swimming towards shore, my creature's consciousness temporarily suspended. It returned in full force when my feet touched sand again. Striding on to the beach, sheets of water dropped from me, and the undertow from a retreating wave sucked at my legs. I ran up the sand in the style of a lurching animal. I shouted into the wind, 'aaaahyaaaa,' and felt stronger than I ever had.

I was caught as I crossed the road. The surf club's truck thundered past, pushing me back into the undergrowth.

But I was spotted by the president who saw in me a potential capable hand.

'What the hell are you doing?' he yelled as the truck reversed dangerously back up the road.

'Been swimming,' I called.

'You've been what?'

I didn't reply. In this crisis situation he only wanted to hear his own voice loud and querulous. The blokes on the back of the truck were laughing outright and I zeroed in on the juniors sniggering.

'We need your help,' the president said. 'Get dressed and we'll meet you at the river.'

I nodded and tossed my towel over my shoulder. As the truck sped off I heard 'Fuckwit' shouted from the truck. I gave them the thumb in case they were looking back, and crossed the road.

My mother met me in the hall outside my room. 'Your father can't understand why you won't help,' she said.

'I don't understand either,' I said, and I didn't. I was still too busy speculating on how easy it is for a hero to fall from grace. The bastards accept you and feel they're doing you a favour, and then if you don't continue to conform to their expectations, they give you the arse instantly.

'It's not fair on him,' she said.

'Yeah, he has a really tough time.'

'He cares about you.' I had always thought he had, but if he really cared he would be talking to me, not having my mother fire the bullets.

'Why isn't he saying all this? Every time he talks to me he tells me what an arsehole I am.'

'He feels you're not learning anything, not listening to him.'

'And he knows it all, eh?'

'He's done a lot for you.'

'That means he knows everything?'

'He wants you to help here. He says you can really be a big help. He doesn't understand you running off like this.'

I laughed. *Running* was one of the key words that parents threw at kids who were looking around. I knew it was supposed to trigger an emotional response so the parent could win, you know, shake their heads, throw up their hands: 'How can anyone argue with such childish responses?' OK I had cooled that one and my parents didn't even know yet.

'Don't forget it was me who warned that this would be happening. I'd say it was Dad and the judge and the Squadron Leader who ran out on this one a few days ago, remember? Did they want to do anything then? Not a chance.'

'Talk to him, for me. Explain that to him.'

'Hell that's not what it's about.'

My mother's eyes were about to brim with tears. Her face had become mobile, her mouth tightening in a line as if she were holding back so much pain, and it was all my fault. Her lips began to tremble then. I shook my head.

'I'll be going up on one of the trucks,' I said.

She turned her head away with quick disgust. 'I don't know why I ever had you,' she said with quite venomous disgust, and walked away.

Gillian's door was open and her face appeared around the side of it, smiling. I looked at my mother's retreating back, shrugged my shoulders and turned to Gillian. She opened the palms of her hands and put her head to one side. 'I see you have a problem.'

'I've got a ride up to the fire, so I'll see you later.'

'I'll be making tea and scones, or serving them, up at the hall. It seems it's going to be my career.'

'What is?'

'Serving people.'

'No,' I said shaking my head and laughing.

'I know it's not going to be, that's why I'm going to Uni.'

'You still reckon you've passed?'

'Sure do! How about you?'

'Yeah, I know I have, but it means I don't escape like you. My father's got real plans for me. He's been drilling it to me for years. We both pass, you get freedom and I get to live somebody else's life — well, the life they want for me.'

'I don't see that happening.'

The surf club truck was still at the river where there seemed to be a general marshalling area. Nobody had quite decided what to do with the heroes of beach and surf: they didn't have a water tank, just willing hands and wet bags. Not much defence against an eighty mile fury. I jumped up on the tray to watch the other trucks filling. Their occupants were fire veterans. They were dirty as hell, red-eyed and weary. They must have been in the hills mopping up when the wind changed. In contrast to the farmers, the surfers were tanned, clean and bouncing with energy and keen comments. The president was negotiating for his team with an efficient-looking bloke who talked with his hands on his hips. They were close to a new CFA truck. The president was desperate to get his boys to work because such a volunteer act would help secure government grants for surf clubs, if favourable reports were forthcoming. El presidente returned with orders that they should show up in the western sector where the toughest work was going on: some of the firefighters had received burns during the night and they probably needed replacements.

It was pleasant sitting on the tray, back to the cabin, watching the track to the west being whisked away behind me and the trees bending into the wake of air behind the truck. I realised I had jogged along here. Then we passed the spot where the farmer and his mates held their sporting activities. I wondered if any of the trees would burn. It seemed ridiculous to be heading into a north wind, even though we were on course to circle away from the fire front. When I stood up, holding on to the cabin of the truck, I saw that heavy ribbons of smoke lay over our path through these foothills. The track was sandy, making the truck relatively quiet as we sped along without the hum of tires. Overhead the branches were lower, almost sweeping the cabin roof. I sat down again. The club members were quiet, not sure what to expect; the camaraderie that usually developed in moments of excitement and unease before a surf carnival, or occasionally during a rescue, was strangely absent. So we were a bunch of young men sitting there on a truck, all sprawled legs and arms, watching the scenery pass, and the rest of them at least, not knowing what to expect. I thought I could enlighten them, tell them a few of the fundamental rules of survival in a fire. And then I realised suddenly that a forest fire, no matter how small the trees — this was a pygmy forest, no tree on this sandy soil more than thirty feet — was beyond my knowledge. I only knew about fires that raged in grasslands.

The truck dashed into a clearing around a big dam where a dozen other trucks were being filled by scores of men, filthy with ash, working to control snaking hoses. Pumps on the truck trays were roaring. The red dirt sides of the dam were slicked as if a rain storm had recently blown over the clearing. Our truck braked violently and the club members were caught grasping for holds. Nobody took much notice of them. The president leapt from the cabin and yelled, 'Who's in charge here?' to no one in particular.

A tall thin man of fifty approached the truck walking stiffly as if he was having trouble staying upright.

'You shouldn't have come mate, you can't help us here. You've got no water. It's fuckin' dangerous without water; it's fuckin' dangerous anyway.'

'You can't use extra blokes?' The president was incredulous.

'You mean spread them round a bit?'

'Yeah.'

The tall man looked over his shoulder. He waved a bloke over, and I saw it was the laconic one I had talked to yesterday. 'You wanted someone didn't you Jack, for the other hose?'

'Sure,' Jack said. He looked at me and asked if I could use a hose. I nodded, glad that I would at least be able to hose myself down if the fire caught us. Bugger wet bags mate. Only very limited value in them.

I jumped from the tray and walked with Jack across to the dilapidated heap of red metal and told the three others draped over the rail of the truck that I was going with them. They weren't that interested, so without greeting them I climbed onto the metal tray and leaned on the railing at the back of the tank where there seemed to be a spare hose. There was a whopping big pump whining away and four hoses wound from four outlets. Jack turned away to haul their refilling hose from the dam. The sucking end, with its small brass cage designed to stop muck blocking the pump, was handed up to be tossed into the tank on the tray. I saw the club truck reverse away and turn for the track back to town. I pointed at it, as if the gesture might stop it, and Jack, who had placed himself behind the driver's dented cabin, mistook the gesture and yelled, 'They shouldn't have come out here without water.' I was shocked by the sudden loneliness of losing transport to home and safety. I also realised that these bastards were serious about fighting the fire. I had thought secretly that I would hang around on the club truck until the end of the day. I thought of Gillian, and how stupid I was to leave the relative safety of the guest house and the friendly balm of its showers.

The bloke standing at the other side of the tree held up the brass nozzle with an upward thrust and showed me how to work it. He turned the nozzle, directing the spray away from the back of the truck. After a second, he twisted the nozzle closed and kicked the pump motor to idle.

I grabbed the iron retaining rail as the truck lurched away from the dam. Gallons of water sloshed from the filler openings at the top of the tank. It still splashed about when the metal covers were slammed shut. The truck turned and lumbered over a soft track heading north. The smoke thickened the moment we left the clearing. Occasionally it was so thick that the cabin six yards away was obliterated. I felt I could panic easily. I yelled forward to Jack, 'Have you seen the fire?' and almost gagged at the rawness in my throat. I thought he yelled NO, but I wasn't sure.

I watched Jack dip a handkerchief in the tank and squeeze it out. As he pushed away from the rail with the balance of a horse standing on a bridge it knows is only a deception in space, he tied the handkerchief around his head. Occasionally the smoke cleared, which gave me an idea that the conditions mightn't be as bad as I was beginning to expect. I tried to inspire myself with thoughts of saving Gillian and the town, but hero anticipation and fantasy were both at dead level — I had too much experience with fires. I think I must have been showing my fear because Jack came to the back of the truck to tell me what was happening: the smoke was blowing in from the burning stand of timber on the flat country over which the firefront had passed a couple of times.

'It's not too dangerous,' he told me shaking his head from side to side as if he thought I might not have heard the words over the ever-increasing wind. I nodded, my eyes watering. I thought of the profound coolness of the ocean's swaying depth.

The bloke opposite me was George, a fat little turd I'd seen plenty of. His type lived off the country and had an incredible cunning when it came to hunting without effort: sly traps and a knowledge of explosives, which caused the muffled booms you'd occasionally hear down the far bends of the river. You'd know it was some bastard like him collecting the big Murray cod that were stunned or mutilated by the blast and floating in the slow current. Yeah, so good'ay George, and if you try to take any of the piss out of me you'll cop a fist full of fives. Len was opposite Jack at the front of the tray. One of the blokes that liked being close to the strength, always grinning and fawning, but as dangerous as a Queensland heeler. Turn your back for an instant and you'd be playing buggery. I discovered in the first few miles that, despite the faded CFA painted in large letters on the door, it wasn't an official CFA truck. Jack had bought it as a farm unit when the CFA had bought a new one.

The soft rhythm of the truck on the sandy track was similar to the movements of a motor launch on a day of mild swells. The rest of the crew seemed satisfied. They were leaning back, swaying against the rail and yelling amiable abuse at each other with the easiness of good mates. The thick smoke now directly north had a dense and brilliant whiteness; it could have been a distant sea fog being cleared by the rising sun.

I discovered that the crew were undecided as to where they should begin work because they found themselves on low ground that had been scorched so quickly that clumps of the light grass were still smouldering. The smoke was blown from the clumps into clearly defined streams, like water running down a glass pane. The truck passed through the streams that were low to the ground, some of them gently bulking in front of the vehicle. But the clumps had nowhere further to burn, and would be out in minutes. I looked around furtively, wondering if I'd catch sight of the travelling flame that would have been through here only minutes before us. The driver swung the door open and leaned out with one hand still on the wheel.

'Where the hell is all that smoke coming from?' It was like rising fog filmed in slow motion. He gave a quick look round to gauge the group anxiety and then advanced across the burnt ground towards the source.

I forced myself to breathe slowly as the truck entered the wall of smoke. I was momentarily blinded, my eyes streaming, and the membrane at the back of my throat threatened to close and gag me.

Inside the smoke the light gradually filtered through enough to give the texture, but not the taste, of medium fog. Small flickering flames appeared like torches in a regular line. Greedy little fires were eating at fence posts where wire had once been threaded. I caught the image of a Gothic horror story where steps to a sacrificial altar were lit by oil-filled lamps. Jack drenched the posts as we passed, but then gave it away. They were already too burnt to be used again. There was something indecent about such insidious flickerings — like ants attacking helpless soft-bellied creatures.

When the smoke parted, blue sky was above us. It gave a clue to how close we were to the flames — thick smoke close to the ground can be parted by the mildest swirl of wind. Moments later we could see yard-high flames like an horizon through the fog.

'It's burning back against the wind,' Jack yelled down

to the driver. The fire could only feed on the dry grass to the north and, like a determined animal, was doing so under difficult conditions. It was ripping away using the wind as bellows.

The driver swung open the door and emerged from the cabin again. His left leg was holding the accelerator. 'I think there's a car over there,' he called to Jack, pointing to the northwest where the smoke was thickest.

'Can't see a bloody thing,' Jack said, 'But check it out.'

The driver crouched into the cabin to spin the wheel. Wind lifted the smoke and we saw the car and two figures close to it, working on the flames. That scene was obliterated by a twist of blacker smoke uncurling as quick as a burning snake.

'There's cows there,' the driver said over his shoulder, the shudders of the steering-wheel racking his body.

'Well get the fuck over there, Col,' Jack said. The truck burst through the smoke and the thin, high line of flame, and then pulled into a shallow turn on the untouched ground.

It was a pathetic sight. Two dairy farmers, a slight man and a woman of mammoth proportions, were waving wildly at us. As we came in close the man called for the wirecutters. To the north we could see the cows packed into the corner of the paddock. As the cutters were tossed down, and the man ran to cut the fence, the big woman lowered her arms, holding one corner of the car cushion she had been using on the flames. The fat on her arms hung down like slack balloons.

As we veered into the line of fire we turned on our hoses. Feeling mine stiffen in my hand, I thought, wow, just like my rod.

We sped along the flame line with the four hoses working from one side of the tray, I expected the truck to keel like a boat with an unbalanced cargo. In ten minutes we had extinguished about a mile of flame front and the truck doubled back to soak the area again. The flame would have been a bastard if the wind had changed. It would have angled away to the hills on an unburnt path. It was all pretty sinister. Even if the town was saved by a wind change, this sort of haphazard burning would still put us at risk.

The farmer didn't show much gratitude when we drove back.

'Some rotten fuckin' bastard started this,' he began yelling. 'Mavis saw the cunt. Down our back paddock he was runnin' through the trees. I would've got the bastard but I had no fuckin' ammo for the Three O. Jesus Christ I'm gunna murder him.'

'Yeah, well you get him,' Jack said strangely unsympathetic. Mavis was shaking. She walked towards the car to sit in it. 'Your misses OK?' Jack asked.

'Fuck her,' he said. 'I'll cut the bastard first.'

'Yeah, well we've gotta be going,' Jack said. Col moved the truck off slowly, the water sloshing audibly.

'We saved that bugger,' Jack said. 'It didn't look bad but it would have melted the tits off his cows. If they'd pressed up like, instead of running, they'd 've got their guts barbecued.'

'What about the bastard that started it?' I said, 'What about him?'

'Yeah, well we don't know that do we?'

'I've got a fuckin' good idea,' I said. Nobody said anything. I had heard a conspiracy of silence before. A short way across the paddock I found myself humming tensely as I bumped my heel against the upright of the metal rail. I didn't have any friends on this fuckin' truck. We emerged onto a high gravelled track and Jack and Col were yelling back and forth about whether to refill the tank from a bore in the paddock we were passing, or return to the dam. 'There's no gate along here,' Col called up.

'Bugger that,' Jack said. 'This is an emergency.'

Looking at Jack's grin I began to think that the bastard enjoyed emergencies.

'Alright,' Col said, 'but we left the cutters back with the other bloke.'

'We've got pliers,' Jack said.

Col seemed to be against casual but legitimate vandalism. He drove down the road several miles looking for a gate, but then turned, reversed savagely onto some rough ground, and swung the heap into a tottering half-circle. As we drew opposite the bore again, Jack jumped off the tray and wordlessly held his hand up for the pliers. He cut the five top wires and motioned Len to jump down and help him stand on the bottom strand so the truck could pass over. Col sneered at his concern for the remaining wire. 'Shit, eh,' he said as he drove over the strand.

The windmill sail was racing erratically. The recent winds had damaged the unit so that water was no longer entering the pipe, but spraying in a thirty yard arc. Jack jumped from the truck and stood in the spray; the rest of us followed him. Out of the spray, I could feel the heat dry my clothes and skin instantly.

'We'd be pretty safe here,' Col offered, and I realised we had a problem.

'What's wrong?' I asked Jack.

'This silly bugger got us lost,' Jack said with a yell.

'Bullshit,' Col defended. 'We were all in it.'

George broke up any further apportioning of the blame. 'Look at the bloody mill,' he yelled laughing. The frame was shivering dangerously in an effort to keep the sail from climbing off into the air. The rudder had broken loose and was flailing ineffectually. Several steel legs were tugging at loose brackets on the squares of concrete at each corner of the tower.

'Looks like a sheila in high heels,' George said glancing

around slyly to see if anybody shared his lusts.

'Jesus fucking Christ,' Jack said turning away, shaking his head.

'I wouldn't put my old fella anywhere near that,' Col said looking up at the whirling blades and touching himself.

'Let's get the fuckin' tank filled,' Jack said. They took the sucking hose with the great brass filter and threw it high into the tank. The engine was kicked into gear and Col and Len, despite the fog of smoke, lit up their fags.

I caught the sudden stillness first, and then the quick glances.

'Hey Jack,' Len said. 'He's comin'.'

I turned to look through the smoke. There was a figure two hundred yards away through the smoke haze. Jack was high on the edge of the tank and he jumped down wiping his hands on the seat of his strides.

'You'd better piss off,' he said to me. 'Not worth staying around.'

'Oh yeah, and where am I going to run to?'

'It doesn't matter. If you stick on the roads somebody will pick you up.'

'No,' I said. 'I'll stay.' I went to the truck and took an axe from behind the tool box.

'Now, Jesus,' Jack said. 'You'll have to lay off, he's a mate of ours.'

'That right?' I said. 'You have great fuckin' mates.' Using the back of the axe I swung it hard against the fender of the truck.

'Hey cut it out!' Len said.

'I fuckin' will too!' I said. George was looking cunning and so I glared at him hard to let him know that I knew what he was about. There was an undeniable purpose building up in me. I was clear and determined. This action might be out of character, but I could feel everything in me supported it. I turned to Jack.

'If that fuckin' bastard comes in here, I'll bury this in his head.' Jack walked out to the figure. He met him about seventy yards out. They stopped there to talk, the smoke cutting them from view every now and again. The farmer pointed in at the truck and Jack pointed west. It was a determined conversation, but it was taking too long. I began to stride out, the axe handle across my body and the axe head at my shoulder. It was sharp as shit too. Bushmen keep their tools in really good nick, it can save hours of work. Jack turned around and held his hands up.

'Hold it,' he said. 'Just stay there, no fuckin' further.'

'Tell him to piss off then,' I said. There were a few quick words and the farmer walked off to the west. I waited for Jack about fifteen yards out.

'Are you bloody mad?' Jack said. 'He could take you with or without that axe.'

'He didn't seem to want to.'

'Now look,' Jack said. 'He's in a bad way, he's nearly been burned a couple of times. He's been running. I told him we couldn't take him in unless you said yes. Now how about it? He reckoned he'd go and see the cops if we took him into town.'

'Jesus! He's been lighting these fires.'

'He reckons it wasn't him.'

'We're headed straight into town?'

'Sure.'

'I thought we were fuckin' lost.'

'He knows the way back onto the main road.'

'Alright, but I hang onto this.'

'He'll go in the cabin with Col. You won't see him.'

'I don't fuckin' like it though.'

'It's OK, we'll meet him at the gate over there, he'll get in with Col and that'll be it.'

With the tank full and slopping as the truck crawled across

the broken surface of the paddock, each of us settled back into our corners on the tray. We were headed west and the vehicle slowed awkwardly to pick up the insane bastard of a farmer. He looked at me as he swung into the cabin. His face was blank, although it had the texture of a side of beef under the red light in a butcher's window. One of those farmers who keep their strength until well into their sixties because they never stop chopping trees or lifting livestock. Still, a keen axe could do a great deal to the strength of flesh. He looked through the back window and his eyes were as bright and expressionless as black buttons. I didn't feel too good. I wanted to run up the side of the tank and let him have it with the axe through the back window. I could almost feel the movement beginning but the smoke came down thick then, and I lost sight of him. I strained to hear whether the door opened, for I knew the bugger would be onto me like a cat suddenly plumbing a goldfish bowl. The smoke became noticeably thicker and there was a new taste to the burning. Jesus this whole thing had been a grotty mistake. That bastard in the front thought he'd been badly done by, so thousands of poor bastards pay for it in anxiety and loss.

'There's the highway,' Len yelled.

'YAHOO,' from Col as he spun the heap up onto the road, water splurging over us from the top of the tank. A second later I knew it was a bad find. Rounding the next bend we hit the black smoke. The truck braked and swerved and a wave rushed from the newly filled tank, splashing over the cabin. The wind was a roaring menace, but then I knew it wasn't the wind but the roaring of flame.

'We're on the bastard!' Jack yelled. 'Back up for Christ's sake!'

'Can't see a fuckin' thing,' Col yelled, but he began a cautious backing turn. I began to understand what it would be like to bake. I almost jumped from the truck to run for it. And then a flip of air tossed the smoke away and there, at last, was the horror: an orange wall of flame higher than the truck and moving with the speed of water from a race. The road was no more barrier than a wire fence. My heart began to pound with such an uncontrollable tripping that I thought of metal fatigue. The truck finally pointed in the right direction and I felt marvellous relief. The smoke had dropped over the flame again and for some ridiculous reason it seemed like a barrier: if I can't see it, it doesn't exist. I saw then how most people developed and appreciated such reasoning.

The smoke became thick enough to keep the truck at walking pace, and Col, surprised that he had been the pivot of a successful retreat, thought it might give him some leverage to assume authority. He twisted out of the truck again and asked Jack to walk in front of the truck — he needed a guide.

'Get fucked, Col,' Jack said.

Within a couple of minutes the smoke became a light haze and the truck reached cruising speed. The wind had changed and I thought, well that bloody lot'll go down to the sea.

At a bush track that straggled up to the highway, Col pulled in beside another truck. The crew had seen a lot of work and under the dirt their faces were strained. They hammed it up with the beer they were drinking, but then tossed across a couple of bottles. 'Struth,' Jack said. 'Some blokes come equipped.'

'Not much we can do now,' the other driver called across, but the last word had a rising inflexion.

'We could follow it down,' Jack said.

'Yeah,' the driver said leaning out, his arm pressed to the door of the truck was a thigh of a porker. 'But we don't wanta get caught in any fuckin' blow back. We've been in it already. It crosses the fuckin' road like snakes and ladders... There's gotta be a tunnel in the hills that turns a northerly into a westerly.' I could see the back of fuck-features' head and I knew then that I had a distinct penchant for the homicidal.

'We reckon we haven't seen anything like it,' George said and tipped back his bottle.

'You blokes wouldn't know what happened in Kennedy's Creek?' Jack asked.

'No one's been in there we've seen,' the driver said and coughed. 'It mightn't be there any longer.' It sounded to me as if the fire might have settled an old score for the driver. It wasn't too different from the attitude of the bloke who might toss a butt out a car window at a strategic point, hoping for a holocaust. It was bloody obvious that people enjoyed violence, whether they were starting it or participating in the quelling of it.

'Well we're pissing off,' the other driver said and hurled his bottle into the scrub where it would lie reflecting heat for the rest of the summer and where, just possibly, it would be the source for the next fire.

Jack decided they would follow the road down to the sea, avoiding any short cuts where undergrowth brushing the side of the truck might tempt the fire to bake us. Immediately we entered a scene of devastation. It reminded me of the film *All Quiet on the Western Front*, in which shabby armies had crawled and fought over plains of blackened mud webbed by lines of twisted barbed wire and the silhouettes of shattered heavy guns. Here the trees on the roadside were still smoking against a background of black paddocks chafed by a whirling grey wind. Two burnt-out cars were on the shoulder of the road. That last decision to park safely off the road had been made while each of the families had been fearful but living. They were now lying on the singed earth like huge white grubs that had emerged from the black surrounds. The flames had gone quickly: small eucalypts were still blowing profusions of green, like grotesque topknots. The bodies were curled, every vestige of clothing burnt from them. The heat had distorted limbs unnaturally. A woman still clasped a baby to her chest and another lay at her feet. Her arm appeared to be still reaching for it. She must have lost hold of it and turned for it again.

The males of the family had made it further. The two husbands were at the roadside fence. An assortment of sons lay at the heels of their fathers. The bastards had deserted their women, and the women had died with their babies. I was struck by the incredible injustice of it all, and by the thought of those moments of human terror, when children are exposed to desertion.

A bush was still burning. Jack turned his hose on it. No one spoke. I felt the axe in my hand. The knowledge of it simply arrived in my consciousness. I hefted it and turned to the truck. The farmer was on the tray ransacking Len's lunch tin. He stopped motionless with a sandwich in his mouth. I lowered my eyes and the axe, as if I was overcome by the sight. But it had been my look that had stopped him, and even though I walked to the truck with lowered shoulders and a slight stagger, he was away and running, crashing across the knapsack sprays and over the end of the tray. Why the hell was I always surprised by the speed of his movements? I was running too, but he was off up the road before I reached top speed and I knew I would never catch him while I was carrying the axe, and that I wouldn't want to when not carrying it. I ran back to the truck. 'We can catch him in this,' I said.

'Bullshit,' Jack said.

'Fuck you mate,' I said, swinging the axe and cutting the parking light from the top of the fender. I turned to him with the axe-head poised.

'Alright you prick,' he said.

'What do you mean *I'm* the prick, that bastard up the road is responsible for this, for Christ's sake!'

'We don't know that.'

'It's a good fuckin' bet he is.'

'He didn't say anything to me. Did he say anything to you Col?' It was done in real smart arse style.

'If you don't get in this fuckin' vehicle and move it, I'm going to cut this fuckin' truck up.'

Jack heaved himself slowly into the cabin. I walked around and ducked in the passenger side door. He was cunning though. He saw the second I cooled down.

'He's a friend of ours,' he said. 'He's also bloody dangerous, and I reckon the best shot would be to go to the nearest cop shop. Would you reckon that's OK?'

I looked at him as the mind behind my eyes began reasoning. 'That's OK, sure,' I said.

'Fuck,' he said. 'I'm glad we agree on something.' He slipped the truck into gear and we jolted off.

'Kennedy's Creek' Jack said. 'We'll go there.'

The tentacles of the fire that had crossed the road seemed to be about three yards in width and they had been thorough burns. A scorched earth policy on the part of providence. We turned off the main road and ran through untouched green country for five minutes. The first indication that Kennedy's Creek might be a bummer was a house that was intact despite the black blanket that swept over the galvanised iron fence and across the garden. That small reach of fire had come from nowhere. There'd obviously been a big blaze to the west and the turbulent winds it had created for itself had carried burning rubbish, leaves, smouldering animal dung, and placed it strategically to put the fear in the farm dwellers there.

'You can't tell? eh' Jack said, and I thought, how could that be part of the grand design?

The truck bucked over a railway crossing, the guide rails blackened and smoking.

At a road junction on the outskirts of the town, we came upon a policeman with his jacket open, his tie loose, and his hat discarded. He was standing in the centre of the junction directing traffic, his bike leaning on an untouched telegraph pole. The traffic consisted of one truck, ours.

'Here's your copper,' Jack said. The sweating man waved them on and Jack revved the truck to obey the gesture. As we slowed the cop became furious, his arm gesturing with exaggerated speed.

Len's head appeared at the driver's window. 'The stupid bastard reckons he's at the corner of Swanston and Collins.' It seemed out of courtesy that Jack drove through the junction and stopped. 'Here's where you get out, mate,' Jack said.

'But the bugger's off his rocker.'

'That's your problem, you wanted a copper and we said OK; that's the finish.'

'I said the cop shop.'

'Well you wait there for him if you like.'

'He's the only one in town, right?'

'Sure is. Should be a lot of help to you.'

'Fuck you,' I said, descending.

'Tell the silly bugger,' Jack began as I slammed the door, 'that you know who started the fire. He should know what to do.'

The truck drove off leaving me distinctly exposed. The copper eyed me warily as I approached him. He began buttoning his coat. I opened the conversation cautiously.

'There's some bodies that need some attention back on the highway,' I said.

'On my bloody bike,' the copper screamed, his coat blowing open in the wind. Then, stunned by his own outburst he said, 'Go directly to the fire station,' as if he were completely in control of the situation.

'Yeah but how ...'

'Are you questioning me?'

'Yes.'

'What right do you have?' His words were calm but his face was brimming with rage.

'I thought you might need to know.'

'Get fucked you little shit,' he said and turned back to his post in the centre of the junction.

'Where's the fire station?' I called after his departing back.

'Find it smart arse.'

I turned towards the town and realised that perhaps the junction was the best place for the town's authority. It was destroyed. Fingers of fire had dashed through the town, taking houses and shops in the rarest of patterns. From where I was walking I could see that on one street only a single house remained, and on another, closer to the open country, only a single one had been taken. It hadn't been the same blaze that had claimed the lives on the main road, for the fire blaze had really ended here. Jesus, I thought, it takes a different path every time. It's boiling away in the hills and it flicks out tongues in every direction. Perhaps the fire had been out to the town on several different tacks. No wonder the copper had retreated to neutral ground from where he would see the first help arriving from the authorities. Why wouldn't a sensible person fall back on a routine he knew best, and resort to the attitude of a petulant child? Those things just might bring relief to someone who had been tipped over the edge by his incapacity to help.

The fire station was burned to the ground, although a great deal of equipment had been heaped on the road in front of it. So there must have been quite a battle to preserve it.

I realised that it wasn't strange to feel isolated, although the feeling had come with the shock of depression. I was completely powerless to reach the security of law and order. For a moment I thought the concept of 'law and order' should be visible like a haven on the landscape. If I'm not careful, I thought, I could easily reach the condition of the copper. Just now would be a great time to be able to conjure up a different environment or a secure position and run and hide in it. I, like everybody else, had a great capacity for delusion.

Eventually I cadged a lift from a passer-by who had to slow down outside the fire station in order to negotiate his way around the heaped equipment. Particularly appropriate for the type of fire being fought today, the manual hose carriages could be used for fighting the fire while running from it.

My new friend — any person was who had a vehicle for out-running flame — was a businessman on his way to Anglecrest to be with his holidaying family. He had been re-routed off the main road by police who had set up a barricade south of the turn-off and had sent him back.

'They had no idea what I should do,' he said as he drove with one hand on the wheel and picked his nose for familiar sensation with the other. 'They just wanted me out of the section they were controlling.'

'Didn't you talk to the copper at the junction out of the town?'

'Yeah, I did, but he wouldn't know which bottle you pissed into.'

'That right,' I said.

The businessman looked grim. He was shocked by the enormity of the damage done to the town, but he wasn't going to speak about it. Admitting to fear might turn his anxiety for his family at Anglecrest into madness.

Groups of people were working on the houses, dragging anything salvable onto the footpaths.

'The phones are out,' he said. 'I tried ringing my wife.' He looked at me to see how seriously he should take this, and it was only then he commented on my filthy clothes and red-eyed face. 'You've seen it?' he asked.

'Yes,' I said.

'How is it? I mean is it really bad.'

'It can be,' I said. 'I think the worst of it is that it doesn't have any rules. There's no logical pattern to it. It can turn anywhere. The winds change, it starts its own winds, and it can come off the main fire in the hills, from any angle...'

'You mean we shouldn't be driving along here; it's not safe?'

'Definitely dangerous,' I answered him, watching to see the effect of this revelation.

'I've never been anywhere dangerous before,' he said. I thought my ashed face must disguise my age or something, and then I thought that now he realised it was serious it didn't matter whom he talked to. He could be frank and open without loss of face. Unfortunately this dropping of image wouldn't carry over into domestic relationships. He would never tell his wife he had never been in danger, and after today he would tell of how he drove through the stricken landscape, just to make sure they were safe. He must have thought confessions were the standard thing because he began to document his innocence: 'I reckoned the police would have actually said something if they didn't think I could get through. They should have said, "Look, it'll be dangerous", something like that.'

I settled back on the seat. 'I had a run-in earlier with the bloke who started the fire,' I said.

He was silent, not wanting to believe me and thinking he had made a considerable error in confiding his ignorance of danger.

'Come again?' he said.

'The bloke who started the main blaze, he was on our truck coming into the coppers but he shot through. I chased him, but the axe slowed me up.' I paused. 'I wouldn't have tackled the bastard without it.' He was silent. If he didn't go on he wouldn't catch me out as a callow braggart. The questions would have to come from him.

'So you're going to the police now?' he asked cautiously.

'I don't think it'll do much good. I'm not going to the locals anyway. He's a good mate of the Anglecrest copper.'

'I don't believe that,' he said.

'What?' I asked.

'That they'd let him go because he was a mate.'

'What about if he was the leading light in the town? What if half the town thought he was a good bloke?'

'They wouldn't believe he did it,' he said as though he didn't believe it either.

'That's right,' I said. 'They probably think that.'

'You reckon he did it though,' he said as an accusation. I could have described a bloke whom he thought a lot of.

'Yeah, I do. Earlier in the week he abducted and assaulted a Jewish woman down here.'

'Hey, I heard about that. But she was pretty unstable though. You know, been in a camp and that, and the Jews are always on about that stuff anyway.'

'He did though,' I said.

'You saw it did you?' he said with an attempt at sarcasm.

'Yeah, I stopped him,' I said. 'He knocked me cold though.'

'Huh,' he said dismissively.

I looked around at him slowly. 'Are you saying I'm a fuckin' liar or something?' He nearly shit himself for he caught the rage in my voice. I was prepared to start shoving him out his door and fuck what happened to the car. I fought against the movement, and at the same time said to myself, there is something wrong with me: I can't compromise any longer. I'm close to some sort of barrier and I keep crossing it to look at the other side. If I cross over, I'm secure in knowing that I'll do whatever I want to. It's also an area that people will respect. They'll tread cautiously when they know I'm close to it. I sat back in my seat. 'I don't want to talk about it anymore,' I said quietly. 'I'm bushed. I'm not myself.'

'Sure,' he said. 'I understand.'

'I get angry too quickly,' I said. 'I don't even know I'm doing it.'

'Yeah,' he said quickly. 'It gets you that way sometimes.'

I could feel him glance at me suspiciously. He thought he had the maniac next to him.

A few miles on he asked me whether I still wanted to be dropped at the police station. He was obviously pretty stupid. It was easy to see that he was still fishing. 'Yeah, you can,' I said. 'If it's still standing.'

As we reached the main road and the last swoop over the river, I saw the town was untouched. The smoke was high, although it was still thick coming down the river valley. He dropped me at the station and shot off. I knocked and went in. The place was empty. The well-worn counter was covered with ash and that hadn't been disturbed for some time. I took a sheet of paper from the desk behind the counter and wrote that the farmer had been coming in with us, but had then decided against it and fled. I signed my name. I put the paper on the desk and weighted it down with the ink-well. Even before I left the office I felt the swirl of hot wind, and then it was inside, stopping my breath with the thickness of smoke and ash that it carried. I was reluctant to leave without getting my story across. I knew the bastards on the truck would have cooked up something. Walking down to the river I got on a truck that was going on up the hill past the guest house. I saw the beach, filled with caravans whose positions seemed hazardous, as the tide was coming in. It looked as if they had chosen to drown rather than burn. I attempted to conjure up a sea of waves meeting a sea of flames. I saw flames scorching water.

At the guest house I jumped from the truck and ran off the road. Further up the hill was a roadblock allowing only fire-fighting units to proceed. The surrounds of the guest house looked as though they had been given a haircut: trees bare of branches, a portion of the hedge laid low and dragged into the vacant block next door. The hundreds of yards of guttering around the roof of the place was brimming with water, dripping onto the verandah. If the fire entered the town with the velocity I had seen the preparations would be useless. It would depend whether the wind dropped in an hour or two, which it usually did in the evenings.

My father was still working with the Squadron Leader. They were both standing back organising the rest of the guest house volunteers. I walked up to them. They were unaware of my approach.

'How far off is the main blaze?' I asked as I walked up.

'It seems to have been coming all day,' my father said.

'If it does come into the town,' I said, 'it'll wipe out half of it. Nothing can stop it. Kennedy's Creek is a mess. It took more than half the town there; you wouldn't believe it. We found bodies north of there on the main road.'

'It's that bad. We heard it was pretty bad, but nothing like that. We should have got out when we could've.' My father's face was slicked with sweat and had paled despite his tan. It had obviously been harder waiting.

'I had a run-in with our old friend,' I said.

Both men were too preoccupied to follow that up, but I persisted. 'He's been lighting fires all across the dairy country north of here,' I said. 'He was coming down with us to turn himself in, but I buggered it up. I saw the bodies of the families and went for him with an axe.' For some ridiculous reason my eyes flooded with tears and I turned away to go into the house. 'This place'll go up like a tinder box,' I said looking back. I felt my father's hand on my shoulder but I shrugged it off. I pretended I was rubbing ash out of my eyes. 'It's bloody bad up there,' I said. 'I think you should be looking at camping on the beach. Jesus, it's so unpredictable.' I could feel renewed tears running in my nose. 'I'm just feeling sorry for myself. I'm going to wash.'

When I ran up the steps to see Gillian, I knew I wasn't that bad. All that stuff could be forgotten in her presence. The house was empty. I could tell by the echoes when I stepped off the verandah. I remembered we had passed the street where the local hall had been mobbed by cars. She'd be there in the best country-woman tradition dealing out tea and sandwiches, and handing out wet towels and burn cream. Damn the stupid bastards. They could look after themselves. It was hypocritical of them to pretend to the women that they were putting in true effort. They were like the men of the family caught in the firestorm who had run, while the women had attempted to cope right through to the end.

It was awful to imagine that I too could have blanked my mind to anything but flight. And yet in imagining it I knew the capacity was there. I knew that I would rather fight next to a woman than a man, in view of the evidence I had seen. Men avoided responsibilities in the name of the image of breadwinner and general know-it-all; while the women were left to cope with home, children and a petulant, indulgent husband. And they knuckled down and did it while the men whined. The men expected a good time forever because they could always lord it around the house when the outside world became a little rough.

There was dust on the hall tables and the wind blasting over the roof gave a high roar. You could hear the house straining to keep its ground. The hot water was a shock. I had expected the house facilities to have failed long before this. But the thought that this house, despite all the chaos I had seen today and all that I expected tonight, was still perfectly functional, gave considerable comfort — even the beginnings of hope. The knowledge came to me then that we could survive the flames and the debilitating machinations that would surround the farmer and his capture. Nothing need change unless I decided not to follow up on the farmer. If I missed doing that, and it seemed that no one else would do it, there would be an unsettled part of me that would undermine some of the good things I had done. I washed my hair under the shower, and dug the ash from under my nails. I'd be the cleanest fuckin' firefighter in the town. I was tempted to leave myself pretty dirty, but I realised that it would only be affectation, and I was beyond that now. Not half fuckin' bad, I thought. I'm going to participate in this hell tonight with a strong mind and a strong body: I'm someone worthwhile. Marvellous how clear-headed a strong hot shower can make you.

On the way back to my room I heard Hans and Rachel come into the hall. They were arguing. 'I told you it was so close,' she said.

Hans was remote. 'It is not bad,' he said. 'We are close to the water.'

'How can you not take notice of me?' she said. 'I know the feeling of such things.'

'There was nothing to be done, whichever way it was.'

'But if I am telling people things I know, you should support me.'

'You are not always right,' he said.

'I'm more likely to be right about such things.'

They obviously thought they were alone in the house.

I wanted them to keep talking. Perspectives from such experience were rare. People without experience tended to confuse themselves with elaborate logic. I had decided my parents did that, the way they had ignored the possibility that the keen personality around town, Farmer Larra, could be responsible for the fire. If I had mentioned the possibility to Rachel she would have understood me instantly.

'I knew,' I heard Rachel continue, 'as soon as I smelled the smoke ... like the ash dust in the compounds. And now all these poor people are stuck here.'

'They wouldn't have been able to leave the town. I didn't want them too upset.'

'Some will be burned,' she said. 'People always try and save possessions. They think that they are part of their possessions, that if they lose them they are not quite right anymore. It is such rubbish. But I couldn't tell them that. You didn't say that I would know.'

'I didn't know.'

'You listen too much to people like the judge. Those people are not to be trusted, they think that laws are for an ordered life and that everybody who follows them is alright. It is not so at all.'

I pulled on my shoes, tied them and walked up to their room. Rachel's voice was becoming harder.

'It is not forgivable for you to say that I'm so upset because of that man. It frightened me yes, but these things go along with knowing what is about to happen. If you are not frightened you are not knowing what is about to happen. You must always listen to your fear.'

Hans's response was weary. They had obviously worked their way over similar ground before. 'I should not have done this,' he said easily.

I knocked on the door. There was a moment of silence

before Hans asked who it was. I imagined him moving quickly to the door with a heavy object in his hand.

'It's Jim,' I said. 'I've just seen Larra.'

Hans opened the door and stepped back to ask me in. They evidently had swift visual communication for I knew that without a nod from Rachel, he wouldn't have asked me into the room.

'Where have you seen him?' she asked. She was bending over a suitcase on the bed. Hans had a wooden coathanger in his hand.

'At the back of the town. He was coming down to see the police.'

'See the police...' she said, 'That is wrong. That man would never come to the police. He will kill first, kill himself.' She put her finger to her head in a very uncharacteristic gesture and made a sound like a child imitating the popping of a gun. 'That is what he would do.' I had never imagined an adult, especially her, mocking suicide, but I knew that she had every right to be so casual and dismissive of death. 'He will be back,' she said. 'It is good to be cautious you know.'

I told her I agreed and said that I thought the things happening to him up in the hills could only make him more determined to act against the people who had been involved in his having to leave the town.

'He is a very dangerous man,' she declared, and closed the suitcase as a gesture that I should leave.

'I thought I should let you know,' I said. I decided not to say that I had run at him with an axe because I saw that they would regard such a statement accurately: as a rather boastful disclosure. People of their experience would not need to embellish. The story shouldn't be told if it had no relevance or conclusion. As I left the room I thought, well I did chase the bastard. It had not been from courage, but out of spontaneous fear and hate, and there is very little courage in that. It only meant that I had the capacity to carry such emotions strongly. As I left the room I said that it looked as though we'd be spending the night on the beach.

'Have you seen the beach?' Hans asked. 'How do you say ... every man and his dogs are there.'

'With the wind,' I said, 'it's not going to be that safe unless you're in the water, although a sea breeze comes in most evenings.

Gillian walked through the gate into the grounds of the guest house as I was walking down the verandah stairs. She ran up and hugged me. I couldn't believe that I deserved such spontaneous affection; our physical contacts had taken place mainly at heights of lust.

'Where have you been?' she asked, stepping back.

'On one of the trucks. We only just got back.'

'Come and watch from the beach,' she demanded with an enthusiasm that startled me. 'It's fantastic.'

'What do you mean?' I asked as she led me by the hand.

'You'll see,' she said. 'I haven't seen anything like it. Walking through the smoke in the crowds of people is like a wild dream. You know, you're suspended as though you aren't really part of it.'

The dunes were hotter underfoot than I had ever felt them. I wondered with what gusto the ti-tree would go up. They were often wet with dew in the evenings but I knew the fire could create its own climatic conditions. For a moment on the top of the dune it was like looking down on cloud surfaces from a plane, and then the wind caught the smoke and pushed it up around us.

'Was it like this in the truck?' she asked.

'No,' I said. 'I was scared most of the time. I saw some families burnt. They didn't have a chance.'

'God,' she said. 'We didn't hear about that at the hall. No one told us.'

On the beach in the thicker smoke, it was like carnival nights. The cars and caravans were lit up for the early approach of evening. We walked down to the water's edge and watched the people walking around in the smoke as if they were at a new picnic ground.

'What's been happening at the house?' I asked.

'Everybody's become an expert,' she said, 'without even having seen the fire.'

I laughed. 'Who's the worst?'

'The judge,' she said. 'He wants to organise everybody, you know: "In the event of the fire approaching the house, we'll all need to know where to go and what to do", sort of stuff. He likes to point: "You go there, and you go over there." Everybody is very polite to him and then plan their own rush to the beach. We watched horrible eruptions tower into the sky and that's something you can't fight with bags or green branches.'

'Yeah,' I said blankly. 'It's hopeless isn't it.'

'Rachel says we should just run . . . if we could.' She laughed. 'God, I agree with her. All the men want to be thought great fighters you know: "I think we should stay and tough it through." It's all so much rubbish.'

'What about my old man?'

'He isn't saying much at all, just working at clearing the rubbish away from the house. He hasn't given an opinion really. I think he just doesn't want us to worry because there's not much we can do about it.'

People began drifting into the shallows, standing knee-deep and looking back over the dunes to the far ranges; the foothills were alight now. I noticed they were mainly fathers, their kids running up to them and playing in the water at their feet. The mothers were busying themselves storing goods or preparing meals in the caravans, content for the moment to let their husbands observe and make decisions. How wrong they were. After seeing how the panicked males had flown, I'd never take my courage for granted again. But how did you warn people? I imagined the panic and the scrambling in the shallows when the flames licked down from the ti-tree on the dunes.

'In an atomic explosion it would be like this,' Gillian said, 'People looking for pockets where they'd be safe.'

'Shit, you're right, and it'd start the same way. Some old man out looking for revenge.'

'Imagine if you were old,' Gillian said, 'it wouldn't matter whether the world went with you or not.'

That frightened me. I tried to think myself into a position where I could end it all for everybody, not just myself, but there was too much I hadn't experienced. I couldn't do that. And was that all that would stop me, a selfish reason like that?

I thought how much this would be Larra's environment. The bastard would be creeping around down here unseen in the smoking night. I would need a weapon, and the shotgun was in my cupboard. Larra wouldn't run from me if I had nothing in my hand to kill him with.

Out to sea, the smoke had been pushed onto the surface by the wind. Our haven out of the wind wouldn't last for ever though. Slowly the light was going and as it did the dark orange glow from the north began to show its fierceness.

'I don't like any of this,' I said to Gillian, 'I can feel the nastiness growing. Things are going to boil over here. I think we should go up to the house while we can and get a shotgun I've hidden.'

'Are you sure?' she said. 'Sure it's necessary?'

'No I'm not,' I said.

'That's alright then, I'll come up. I'm frightened of people who are sure those sorts of things are the answer.' I was sure it was, but was naturally cautious answering direct questions in a crisis, for fear of being caught out. My weaknesses seemed to be multiplying.

We jogged up to the pathway through the dunes, keeping to one side as people were running down to the beach. At the top of the dunes we were almost turned back by the smoke. 'We're OK,' I said, 'until the ash in the smoke is freshly burning.' The road was barely visible and we hesitated to cross. 'Up further,' I said. 'There's a road block and they'll have lights.' I followed Gillian along the side of the road, looking back all the time for cars that might be close to the shoulder of the road. Uniformed police were at the road block but we only glimpsed them. The wind seemed to cease for a moment and I thought, Christ we're going to be alright, and then it began to howl again.

It was an easy run downhill to the guest house. I noticed how strange it was that there was a ceaseless roar of engines yet I couldn't sight a vehicle. We made for the back door and into the hall. Inside the house it was as if there was a steaming process in operation. Smoke rose gently from beneath each closed door. There was no fire yet though; my room was thick with smoke which had merely blown in the seams of the closed windows. The gun was in the cupboard behind my hanging clothes. I grabbed it, broke it and loaded two shells. Gillian watched me doubtfully.

'That could fire off in all the rush,' she said.

I broke the gun open and held it over my left forearm. 'Not this way.'

'It's not right,' she said. 'We shouldn't have to be doing this. I mean having it is only a step away from using it.'

Hefting it like that was strangely comforting. 'It's OK,' I said, 'It'll show the bugger we're fair dinkum.' The barrels were straight and solid in my hand. I felt slightly larger than life. A weapon enabled you to make rather significant decisions, I thought. Outside there were lights turning sharply. A shadow flicked in front of me with the sort of speed with which Larra could move. I took fright and fired both barrels, finding that I had pulled them into the air quite unconsciously as I did so. At least that's where I found them pointing when I looked down at my hands with shock. Gillian grabbed me. 'What the hell have you done?' she shrieked.

'Nothing, I hope,' I said quite calmly, although my senses were grating wildly in an attempt to discover just what had happened.

'Fuck that,' I said at last and threw the gun into the foliage of a tree. Gillian walked warily forward to discover what damage may have been done.

'I fired into the air,' I said. 'I'm sure of it.'

'You're not, you know,' she said turning back. 'You're the classic moron, ready to click into gear at the slightest excuse. God, he hasn't done a damn thing to you.'

'I chased him today,' I said. 'I saw the families and saw him eating there on the back of the truck and I went for him.' I shook my hands at chest level. 'I would've chopped the bastard into a thousand bits. He really scared me shitless.' At the same time I thought, I wouldn't have shot him just now anyway. I didn't want to. If you've not used a weapon you don't know how you'll react; your range of options is therefore very limited. You don't know whether to fire or call halt, or just hit him with it.

Gillian was watching me with dread. 'You saw him today?'

'Yeah, I did.'

'You didn't tell me.' She thought I was trying to worm out of my panicked action.

'I did though. He was coming down on our truck to see the police. That's what he said. I doubt that he was. I think he wanted to get out of that black country.'

'You mean you know he's down here.'

'No, he ran off about ten miles out I s'pose.'

She walked back to me without completing her check. 'Let's get another weapon,' she said. 'But you'll cause more damage with that gun than he can.' I thought, well she really knows the extent of him; or is that only the extent of him where women are concerned? I took her hand and we ran into the workshop. There was no visibility inside. 'Have you got a match,' I asked, and she burst into laughter. I began to giggle too. It was the hysteria that breaks from you after you've survived a serious accident. I found a shovel behind the door and a saw on the work bench. I cut the handle into two pieces giving each of us a half-yard length of timber. Running back to the beach I had no thought for my parents or anybody else in the guest house. My complete absence of concern puzzled me.

Several flashes of light followed by a boom of the exploding fuel depot close to the showgrounds signalled that the fire was on us. From the beach the burning was so bright that it threw shadows over the dunes. People began to moan.

'Let's get further up the beach and into the water,' I said. 'That next bay is shallow for a couple of hundred yards out.'

'Should we get away from everyone else?' she asked. 'I mean I feel safer here.'

'Sheep always feel safe together. We need to be able to get as far from that fuckin' fire as possible without having to swim.' We had to negotiate the rocks at the point with extreme care. I looked up at the cliffs; their outline against the sky was only intermittently visible through the pouring smoke. Everybody should be along here, I thought. From our new viewpoint we could occasionally see across the main beach to the far hills in the east. The fire front was there too. Even after the prolonged anticipation the curtain of silk flame was an awesome spectacle. It was much higher than the trees it silhouetted before devouring. It seemed to be sucked spasmodically by a high curl of air where what must have been a mild ocean breeze met a northerly. On-shore breezes happen despite strong directional winds.

We were the only ones on this far beach. Long shadows ran from our feet in the cool watery sand.

The approaching brightness was the light of an early summer morning turning yellow. When a house in the hills burst into flames, the beach people groaned like a football crowd. A goal had been kicked by the opposition.

'Is that coming down here?' Gillian demanded, her face slack with fright.

'Hey,' I said, 'How can we see that?' The meaning was slowly clear to my deadened brain. I jumped in the air. 'The fuckin' wind's changed.'

The smoke was cleared from the ocean and the beach and the blackness obscured the naked flames. It was suddenly the long body of a dark and fluorescent caterpillar. 'Shit,' I said. 'We're saved.'

'There's something along there,' Gillian said, and seeing the growing light from the west we walked into the ocean — I loved that water like an old friend. Now we had a clear view of the low hills to the west of the town — Dead Man's Back. Flames were running through the dark trees as if molten metal had been spilled. There had always been something comical about those hills: they seemed the result of a giant comedian's pratfalls, the face buried in a cold soup of sand at the headland, leaving only the back of the head free to merge into the neck and the rounded shoulders. The arm thrown out from the shoulders had a sinister appearance. The hand lay close to the town — the fire's audience in fact — and it had the threatening if-you-don't-laugh-at-me-I'm-going-to-do-something-nasty-to-you closeness of childhood circus clowns.

And now it was about to.

Keeping away from the sea breeze the fire ran down the back of the arm and entered the town. On one house, three figures scrambling on the roof, probably still cleaning leaves from the guttering and stuffing socks in the down pipes, suddenly leapt from their perch. Moments later a dull explosion, a shift in the line of the house, and it was engulfed in flames.

'We should be out further, I think,' Gillian said, pulling me by the hand.

We backed out until we were at waist level. 'We're OK,' I said, 'Unless there is a wind change.' Down on the other beach a large wave struck a caravan, resettling it at an odd angle. When the flames gusted across the road and into the trees covering the dunes, the crowd rushed into the water. Hundreds stood in the shallows as the hot silk billowed higher than any rolling surf, shooting out like air blowing across calm water. In front of us the flames came to the edge of the cliff with a scorching heat. We dunked our heads but were dry in an instant. Bits of burning branches fell from the cliffside to the sand, showering sparks where they landed. More swirls of sparks landed over us in the sea. The heat dried our throats. Luckily the smoke laden with ash and embers didn't stay with us but was squirrelled off down the coast by the wind. We floated in the water, only our heads exposed. We dipped them constantly and turned our faces to the open sea. Around us the water was a translucent orange, the white carpet of sandy ridges below showing light and shadow like a tiger's back. Whenever the heat of the fire altered the wind direction, the smoke shadow gave coolness the way clouds move across land and block winter sunlight. But that was only an impression.

I had no anxiety about surviving — and I'm sure it was more than just not caring whether I survived or not — so I was enjoying myself. It was true that I didn't care whether or not the town was obliterated; I knew I would only care if more children and struggling women were burnt. But that thought stopped my enjoying the warm soup in which I was suspended with another creature.

## CHAPTER 11

The morning light was a revelation. Gillian and I slept fitfully and we were fully awake before the grey dawn. The wind had dropped and the air was hot and smoky. Along the beach it looked like a bombed refugee camp. The odd caravan had been burnt and the others were smoke-blackened. Figures moved slowly around in the early light. The beach sand and the dunes were black. The sea was grey and charred rubbish was already floating there. At the rocks we scooped away surface ash from the pools and washed our faces. Our feet looked as though we had been walking in black sand.

Over the rocks and on the main beach we saw women preparing meals from mounds of bread and tin cans on a trailer. The local policeman was supervising, and when he approached, Gillian left and walked down to the sea.

'They reckon you caught up with Larra,' he said. He was a big fit man under his grimy uniform and I thought, you fuckin' bastard. He must have caught my aggression because he looked down apologetically.

'I know what he's done,' he said. 'At least some of the things. But basically he's a good bloke.' This is the man, I thought, who helped scare a young girl in the name of fun and mateship. He'd say: we weren't going to hurt her, just have some fun, tease her a bit, she would have enjoyed it, you know.

'Do you know any bad bastards?' I asked.

'Larra had a bad time during the war, but he survived. He was wounded an' that. I realise he's got to come in.'

He looked me in the eye with all the directness of an honest man.

'But he's done a lot for people around here, and we don't want to go too hard on him.'

'Yeah, I can see what he's done for people around here,' I said.

'Are you fuckin' joking or something?'

'He wouldn't have done this, no way he would have. That's bullshit.'

'I don't think so, for Christsake we ran into a dairy farmer who said he saw a bloke running through the bush with flame.'

'Yeah, listen that doesn't make it him. I spoke to that bloke and he reckons he couldn't point him out.'

I was silent for a moment looking out to sea, my hands on my hips. Gillian was paddling, kids were chasing each other around the caravans, sandwiches in their hands. I looked back at the copper.

'I know that bloke,' I said. 'I've chased him. He's capable of utter bloody cruelty and you say there's no way he'd do that. You must be bloody mad. He abducted and assaulted a woman from the guest house for Christsake.'

'He'll go for a row on those charges.'

'Are you going to talk to him about the fire?'

I was aware I was being looked at as though my appearance was going to be weighed significantly: after all I was only a kid wasn't I?

'That's how its going to be,' he said walking off.

'You mean no questions?' I said.

'Nothing to fuckin' do with you.'

Gillian was watching the water where dead embers floated like blackened egg shell.

'They don't think it was him,' I said, 'who started it.'

'You didn't think they would, did you?'

I let out a dismal laugh. 'Yes, I did.'

'Just because you guessed it might happen doesn't mean it did happen, in that way I mean.'

'I'm as certain as I've ever been of anything.'

'A judge would have to be absolutely certain before he sentenced someone or he could never do it, and they've made mistakes.'

'In Germany the legal profession went along with the Government. If you were a Jew, or retarded, or crippled, or odd, you were guilty.'

She looked up from the water flowing around her feet. 'And if you were a rapist you were also a firebug?'

It stopped me for a moment, but the old feeling of certainly came back more strongly than ever. 'He did it,' I said emphatically, at the same time knowing I sounded like a geriatic judge rapidly defending in his dotage a forgotten decision.

Farmer Larra's farm had been untouched by the fire although it had come close. It was stupid of me to visit but it had occurred to me that when the bastard had walked out of the smoke to the truck he was relatively clean. Certainly dusted with ash, but he had also been clean shaven and his old army trousers had been pressed. The bastard hadn't been living in the bush at all.

I approached the farm warily. I had dropped off the back of a fire truck that was heading out to drench the countryside with water. With the wind down the truck crews were desperate to put out the thousands of smouldering fires in tree trunks and fence posts that could catch again if fire conditions reoccurred.

I watched the peaceful farm buildings from a stand of green trees. They mightn't have burned, but moving through the undergrowth I was soon black with ash that covered the leaves. The house was small with a red roof and what looked like white painted brick walls. The outbuildings were surrounded by the only trees. The dairy farm stood out like an oasis. The earth was blackened on three sides of it, and the fourth side was ploughed ground for several hundred metres north. That was damning evidence; many farmers made firebreaks to protect their houses. It just looked suspicious. A mill was churning at a happy speed and forty odd cows were grazing in the home paddock. On the way out I'd seen several other farms that had survived, but none seemed quite so pristine as Larra's. Even the cows had been milked close to the routine time. The last of them were moving away from the milking shed. God, had we been taken for suckers. He'd been here all the time. Aaah yes, I thought and what the hell happens now? I inform the local cop and that's the end of it.

I hadn't made a conscious decision to visit the farm, I suddenly found myself descending to the low ground and the dry creek bed to the west. It followed a sort of half circle close to the house. Further up he probably let the dairy effluent into it. I was walking upright so I hadn't completely committed myself to a sneaky approach. I stopped quickly and ran doubled, until I came up behind the dairy buildings. I could hear the sound of a high pressure hose on concrete, so the dairy was inhabited. The motor for the chiller and separator was cranking away. Any noise I made would be covered. I came up close to the top of the bank and peered through the gums.

I couldn't see much in the shadows of the building. I glimpsed the whiteness of splashing water and gum boots walking through sunlight several times, but that was all. From the movements, rather slow and languid, I would have said that it wasn't Larra, but then I had only seen him moving when he was driven by his compulsions. It was conceivable that he liked his animals and relaxed when around them. The sunlight became stronger and completely blanked my vision into the dairy. I debated whether to move down into the water course again and approach the house, or to wait out the dairy worker, whoever it was. At least I had bearings here and there could be no more than two people around the farm. If I waited they'd at least meet up some time, and if there was only one it would be no sense stalking him. Beyond the farm smoke still rose off the hills. A strong and tuneful whistle broke out from the dairy and somewhere I could hear a radio. A gate clanged behind the shed and a bull swung out from around the shed and down the lane to the paddock. He had been cut out so he wouldn't interfere with milking. He let out several obligatory bellows to notify the herd that he was still around for business. Work in the dairy buildings was obviously finishing. A woman walked out of the dairy. It gave me an intense feeling of uneasiness and I pushed down from the top of the bank and looked back along the water course. I would have liked to have turned over on my back, not quite in the style of a dog, but my back needed to be covered. That way I would see everything that approached.

I began to have serious doubts about my sanity in coming here, but I thought: OK I'm here, at least try and pull it off. I twisted again and watched the woman walk into the house, or at least onto the verandah covered in grape vine. I didn't hear a door close. She wouldn't have known I was there though; I was certain of my skill at stalking. I had watched animals with acute senses and whip reflexes, from only metres away. I couldn't see a phone line connected to the house and even if there was, the telephone system had been destroyed by the fire. And then, as I lay there with the sun on my back, I realized that I would only have to hear the slightest sound out of place and I'd piss off, running like a rabbit. It almost made me laugh: what am I doing here? Revenge and justice were fine, and they were obviously strong motivations, but it was bloody dangerous to be where I was.

What buried example was I blindly following? I thought of a long dead uncle who had only just made it back to Australia before carking it. He had fought in Burma and he had brought me presents from the war. Unlike the judge, he had given his away. There had been a Gurkha knife with globs of dried blood on the handle, and an army belt and a tent. I'd thought at the time that my father hadn't been to the war and brought back that stuff for me. And I understood now that the purpose of the gifts had been to humiliate my father, the one who had stayed at home. Was I following the example of my uncle? Had those bloody gifts influenced me? I'd always thought any revolt I had found in myself flowed from my father who had refused to go in for the killing. But here I was.

The uneasy thoughts stirred me to action. I stood up and ran a few metres to a tree whose straggling branches brushed the ground and would allow me to cross to the boxthorn hedge that had been cut, with much work, into an English hedge — very correct and angular.

Beyond that was a building I had taken for a garage or a machinery shed. It was roofed with corrugated iron and walled with asbestos, but when I rounded the end of it I saw that it was in fact a large room with a door raised half a metre off the ground and no windows. There was a padlock on the door, a well-used one of brass. I found a crowbar lying with some shovels and with a soundless bump I broke the catch of the padlock.

Inside it was orderly. A red flag was pinned to the back wall and a swastika stood out from its white circle. Artefacts hung around the walls: rifles, machine pistols and swords removed from their scabbards. A German helmut seemed to have pride of place in the centre of the desk beneath the flag. A German uniform was on one of those shop dummies. There were no mementos from the Allied forces. All German. It was a sleazy arrangement compared to the judge's museum. But this one looked well-used. The books in the bookshelf were worn. I took one down and flicked through it. Larra had marked the photographs in his own style. The corpses being bulldozed into a concentration camp pit all had a red tick. A photograph of some nurses being forced to run in front of smirking Nazi officers were also ticked. The pubic area of each of the exhausted girls had been ringed in red, as had each floating breast. The bastard, I thought, suddenly alert. An empty field glass case had been tossed behind the desk. For a person whose gear was so well displayed, the empty case was an instant warning. The bastard is out there watching, probably surveying the house. I grabbed a bayonet and turned to face the door. Nothing. I thought of loading the pistols, but there was no time. I repressed the larcenous impulse to steal a pistol. Should I run from the door in case he was waiting for me? No, he would have confronted me in that room, his power-base.

I moved quickly out the door and along the hedge to the watercourse. At the road I looked back at the house to see if its appearance had a hint of the type of person it contained. A pleasant, ordinary little house sunning itself. It was only the back-drop of blackened and smoking hills that removed it from a normal reality.

When a truck came pounding down the road I tossed the bayonet into the scrub and thumbed a lift. I half expected the bastard to leer down at me from the window. But there was a bunch of blokes leaning back against the rails yarning, oblivious to the rattling speed of the truck which slewed as the driver stopped to take me aboard. I pulled myself up onto the tray and nodded at the blokes.

'How ya going?' they all said in obligatory greeting and

settled back into their respective conversations.

'Watcha been doin out here?' a short dumpy bloke asked me.

'I was out here on a truck yesterday,' I said. 'I didn't get a look at the extent of it all.'

'Dangerous by yourself,' he said. 'You might think it's all burnt out but it could light up again alright. I've seen big fireballs rolling through burnt country. The wind only has to get enough dried shit together and take it over some slow burning flame and it lights up like a furnace and keeps rolling.'

'Yeah,' I said. 'And there's some places that missed it the first time.'

'Not many,' he said. 'Bloody old Larra was lucky,' he said with affection. 'But it's about time he had some.'

'He's had bad luck then?'

'Well, a bit of trouble, right. Some bitch turned on him. He was giving her some jiggedy jig and she decided she didn't like it. Got the coppers after him.'

'That's bullshit,' I said. 'I was there.'

The bloke looked at me with contempt. 'You're the silly bugger,' he said. 'Larra told us. She saw you and started yelling.'

'She didn't see me,' I said. 'And he grabbed her from the guest house.'

'That's the bloody Jew story, a Jew bitch like that'd tell you anything.'

'You're full of shit,' I said, and turned away.

'We'll see who's right then,' he said.

'What'd they have such a big turn out for when they were searching for him? And the bastard ran too.'

'Those Jews got influence that's all, mate. You gotta make a show before they're satisfied.'

'Jesus, what a fuckin' know-all. And you weren't even there.'

'We'll fuckin' see who's right then.'

'Yeah, we will.'

Not having won the argument decisively he called on his other mates in the truck. 'This is the bastard that dobbed Larra in.'

'Arsehole,' came from a bloke leaning with his back and elbow on the railing. 'Let the bastard walk,' his mate said. 'We don't travel with dobbers.' The butterball leaned around to the cabin. 'Hey Alf, this bloke here wants to get off.'

The truck pulled onto the shoulder of the road, black havoc over all the small hills here. I swung down. 'We'll mention to Larra that you're out here,' said the butterball, and the truck load collapsed with laughter. I gave them the thumb. One of them picked up a heavy ball bearing race and threw it at me. It bounced with sparks on the metal road.

The day was really heating up again although there was no wind. I began walking along the road to town and I had the feeling I was a kid again, mooching along the road, not sure where I was going or whether I wanted to get there, scuffing my shoes and tossing rocks at anything that appeared a target. I speculated about reconstructing myself: to become the mechanical man, with the right bits in the right places, free of doubts. If it all functioned in a dull way, so much the better, I could drift along, enjoying myself and avoiding the things or people that challenged me.

Jogging down from the hills above the town, I saw how easily it must have been for primitive people to believe in the supernatural. This blasted landscape had for years been the hills of exciting greenery we had driven through at the start of the holidays, searching for that first glimpse of the sea. Now it was changed so horrendously, it could only have been visited by evil. And where did evil begin?

Did it start with the wizard who had waved his wand of fire to lay the country to waste, or did it start with those who created the wizard? Did the wizard have responsibility for himself?

It was easy running towards the town. I only had to lift my feet and the downhill gravity did the rest. But I realised that I was sweating too much, and it was still a five mile run in. Through the green patches I slowed to walk in shadow. It was strange that here I smelt real burning. I didn't place much significance on it at first, and I had been through several patches before I saw movement. A small wallaby dragged itself with horrible slowness behind the cover of a bush. I stopped stricken. The undergrowth was full of injured creatures. The birds couldn't fly and the animals crouched in silence. Wallabies and kangaroos were the largest I spotted, but then I noticed the possums. Most were half-cooked and ready to die. Others who could move weren't going out again onto the hot ash. It was clear that although their bodies might be free of the scars of flame, their feet had been scorched, and that they would probably die a longer and more painful death. The mass of silent creatures overwhelmed me completely. I had never felt such pity for anything before. Jesus, I thought, we've done this. We've inflicted meaningless pain. And now they were waiting here uncomplaining, hearts tripping furiously in an attempt to rectify the damage. They crouched without looking at me, the intruder; then some moved one or two steps uneasily. With the backs of their heads towards me, it was as if they were inviting me to move among them delivering merciful death. I had seen domestic stock this far into shock and pain, but it had been unimportant to me. I had seen too many of them killed in such callous ways. But wild creatures had always possessed a shyness, an unobtrusive presence and a beauty of existence I had loved and admired. I would never hunt the poor bastards again. And caught with this compassion, warm tears filled my eyes. I started running again.

A couple of miles from town I was picked up by a truck bringing in emergency supplies of food. The driver was almost silenced by his surroundings. He didn't ask me any questions because he could barely cope with the scene.

'I didn't think anything could be like this in this country,' he said. 'I thought this sort of thing only happened in America.' It was the only comment he made. When he dropped me at the police station he didn't even acknowledge my leaving.

A new policeman sprawled behind the counter. His coat was open and his tie loose. He was speaking impatiently on the phone, answering the queries with a series of unconsidered affirmatives. 'Got to go,' he said decisively and hung up. The phone rang again as he turned. 'Yeah, what can I do for you,' he said, his hand reaching for the phone.

'There's a lot of wild animals half dead — they've been burned.'

'Fuck the animals,' he said. 'We've got missing people.'

'Fuck the people,' I said. He didn't acknowledge the comment, but with the phone to his ear turned his back to me.

I left the station and began the walk back to the guest house. The town had barely been touched by the fire, and apart from the furnace that had blazed on the beach front there had only been two probing fingers through the centre, taking out perhaps forty houses. Looking from the end of those finger sweeps you could see right along a path back into the hills.

Voluntary work still occupied the guest house residents and there were only a few people about. The judge was one of the first I saw. He was shaking his clothes out the door at the end of the hall. He had the dirty pile on his left side and the clean on his right. He could have shaken them in the house, it was already so filled with ash. But I realised it was a matter of where to begin first. Making the first move was all important. But he was looking after himself.

'I was looking for my parents,' I said when he turned towards me.

'They were about earlier,' he said and went on with his shaking. No, I thought, he could never exist with destruction around him. His collection of war mementos was only that, a collection. Not something to be used for emotional gratification, or something on which to hang obsessional behaviour. I was pleased he was there getting his house in order. That clean room would be where they would probably congregate this evening for drinks and a discussion of the day's events. That was the judge's function. His view of the world was that he should maintain order, and to do that he would need order about him. Nearly everybody else it seemed had joined those hundreds of people helping the victims with food, clothes or simple comfort. While I like an idiot had been roaming the countryside in search of explanations. And now I was looking for my parents to tell them of my find at Larra's place, knowing that if I told the senior authority figure here of the Larra collection he would automatically assume the man had similar interests to himself and was therefore someone to be examined with sympathy. And then I saw quickly enough that my parents would assume likewise. Even if sickened by such grisly reminders of how close the world hovered to insanity, they would only see the collection as one of the stabilising elements of the man's life. Why did I need to tell them anything? They would immediately distance themselves from the issue by relating the degenerate collection of political and sexual pornography to the remote interest of a museum curator.

I walked down to the beach. There were families salvaging caravans. The burnt ones were being stripped, others winched out of wet sand. I couldn't offer help there. I watched blackened seagulls squawking in the high wind. The waves sloshed onto the beach under a glistening carpet of thick, wet ash. A storm would clean it up in a day or two, otherwise it would lie around for weeks polluting the river and the rock pools and small inlets, and in a week things from the water would be stinking as they began to die. Now the hills were bare of everything but ash; heavy rain would clog the rivers with black dust, killing all those small creatures that depended on fresh water. I recognised that I was beginning to accumulate the emotional baggage of the pessimist: if this happens then that will happen and then that and then... No fight, no cheek for life, and no cleansing exuberance.

I stood up and walked down to the water's edge. Behind me my footprints were white through the surface ash. And the sand where they were working on the caravans was an island of white in the blackness. In the water the form of a dead bird rose and dropped under the wet ash. Death was always there to be anticipated. And the standard by which you judged a person was how well he or she coped with that. I wondered how many people knew about that sort of coping. Did they give that knowledge to someone else to handle? Or did they merely think they were giving it to someone else, and all the while the grim future was poking away in their dreams, producing the distortions that surfaced in Larra's reality?

I wanted to see Gillian and began trudging through the ash to the river. It seemed to me that young people shouldn't have to begin thinking of death. Perhaps young people were without the capacity to gather emotional memory on the sort of scale that would affect them? Whatever the case, I knew Gillian's presence could temporarily relieve my memories and anxieties. She knew instantly what I was talking about. The barriers hadn't gone up there. Adults on the other hand were forever contriving defences of their prejudices and of their inactivity.

As I left the broad sweep of the black tidal river for the road, I saw some people who actually seemed to be enjoying the clean up work. They had an activity they could do together, and there were even smiles and jokes. I couldn't tell the local home-owners from the holiday-makers, but the scene made me wonder whether their enjoyment wasn't in fact in the destruction of their past.

Gillian was playing with a group of children in the park next to the RSL hall. The older kids were dancing. The small kids were being given turns on the swings. She had taken a radio out through one of the windows of the hall and placed it on an old fruit box. The kids were jumping, laughing and tripping over, in their attempts to follow the beat of the music. But the little figures going in and out of the hall were in a different state. Some of the more burnt and stooped kids were being supported as they walked. Two nurses checked them at the door for their true physical condition.

I sat down against the trunk of one of the small trees in the stand near the hall. Watching Gillian, I glimpsed the woman she would soon become. A marvellous thing. Healthy, genuinely concerned, and willing to give of herself. She would always be able to take people out of themselves. Now she was intent on the children, while still being aware, with quick glances, of what was happening in and out of the hall. After only a couple of minutes she caught sight of me amongst the trees. She waved, imitating the dance she was doing with the kids, and then went back to helping them enjoy themselves. I began to doze there against the tree, hearing the trucks and the voices as if from an immense distance. It wasn't an extraordinarily helpful condition, but it seemed more restful than total oblivion. Gillian's voice woke me and I opened my eyes to see her striding towards me. I hugged her, and the couple of cheeky little kids who had followed her across from the park giggled and yelled at us.

'Are you alright?' she asked.

'Sure am,' I said.

'Where have you been?'

'Out to the bastard's place.'

'If you get into trouble out there it's your own fault.'

'You should see what he's got out there,' I said. 'He's got all this Nazi stuff. You know, a lot of bloody filth. I don't mean *Man Junior*, or stuff like that, but pictures of people's humiliation. And he's marked them with pencil, you know, with a sort of sadistic indulgence — circles around women prisoners' genitals, stuff like that. The bastard's mad.'

'So are you,' she said. 'You can't go poking around like that in other people's houses.'

'You can with bastards like that,' I said.

'Don't be mad,' she said. She wasn't angry about it, just concerned that I should be doing the right thing. But I wasn't sure whether she was concerned about the morals of it, or just the style in which I was doing it.

'I know there's nothing I can do about it,' I said. 'I can just tell what I know. But it's really strange how the police don't want to do anything about him.'

'They don't know about him, that's all. They don't know how to place him or deal with him.'

'You mean he's something new to them.'

'I think so.' Some little kids ran over and began pulling at her hands. There was a rock and roll song on the radio and everyone in the park was beginning to jump around. Gillian smiled down at the little bastards. 'I'll see you at dinner-time,' she said.

'Right,' I replied, and watched her walk back to the

park, an unbearable lust eating away any decisiveness I might have had. Legs like that beneath shorts made my insides melt. Or was it because I had experienced her willingness? However I attempted to explain it, there was the overwhelming knowledge that a woman was a total attraction. And why was that such a relief? More than relief, a freedom. I could have eulogised forever.

My parents had returned to the guest house from their morning of voluntary work. After showering and changing their clothes, they tucked into a good lunch. I told them about Larra's cache of Nazi memorabilia.

'It makes me feel sick,' my mother said with determination, although how she had forgotten that a whole race had been taken over by the obsession for symbols of glory, and for armaments to attain it, I couldn't understand.

My image of the good blokes and the bad blokes was changing: our side had always been portrayed as the victims in that clash with insanity. But now I saw that we had been more than expert retaliators, and no doubt just as guilty of provocation. It was like the clashes with my father: behind his mask of calmness he was waiting to retaliate. Allowing me the full run of my outrage, he would remain silent. He waited like a country in a state of strategic unpreparedness — the result of all the correct attitudes they had adopted — needing only some logical excuse to attack. The slightest threat from an aggressor and they would enter the savagery with relish, replying: 'Go on, show how you are prepared to flaunt your brutality, and when you've made the wrong move, we will crush you.'

How would the true story of this history ever be told, I wondered. The tales of glory are reserved for the victors. But how had it really been? Why hadn't the Allies made a single move against the death camps until after the war? Why had they allowed the horror to exist for that long? Could there possibly have been a keen anti-semitic feeling amongst the Allies as well? How much blame would lie with the people who had known about the camps and yet had hesitated to form a policy, or even an opinion, on those camps? They had spent months on single projects to destroy armament factories, and on the search for new weapons, but in all those years they had made no attempt to relieve the horror of what could only have been, to those bureaucratic hierarchies, a 'doomed race'.

The destruction of waterways and the battles for small islands had been priorities above the destruction of the machinery of the death factories that were rapidly removing a race from the earth. But how long would the annihilation of Allied prisoners have been tolerated? Was it that, confident of the outcome, the Allies had in fact been objectively interested in the German experiment, as a possible guide to the future? After all, it had been years before America had entered the war. Of course, as the judge would have said, 'It's all only a matter of circumstantial evidence.' But I was having my doubts about that sort of evidence; it seemed for the most part to be countered with excuses and camouflage explanations.

My father was silent. The table had drifted off into that suspended state in which everyone is pre-occupied with their own thoughts. That's probably the best thing that families can do for themselves: foster those quiet times when people become absolutely unaware of their surroundings and reach a state close to meditation. It's not a generally recognised state, and some parents, anxious to have their children achieving, chide them for their daydreams. The children, unsure whether their dreams are valid or not, have only guilt connected with the process.

'How does all that change?' I asked.

They shook their heads, knowing, even after those few minutes of introspection, what I was thinking about, for they had been trawling along the same lines.

'If there are always going to be people to develop like that it means that every generation begins at square one.'

'No, I think the world is in a continual state of development . . . aaah, progress rather. Things get better,' my mother concluded lamely.

'It hasn't shown that,' I said. 'It shows it's getting worse. More people are killed and brutalised anyway. Throwing Christians to the lions was just a cheap thrill compared to the camps. I mean the annihilation of a race was a nation's policy. And if one can do it . . .'

'I don't think it's like that at all,' my mother said. 'We're not like that.'

'What about the bloke up in the hills?'

'But he's just a larrikin,' my mother said.

'Is that all you call him.'

'I mean, he isn't in power, we don't have those sort of people in power.'

'I don't know,' I said. It could be we don't know who is in power, the types I mean. They mightn't even know until they've been at the top for a while.

'I think we should go home,' my mother announced suddenly. It was a great suggestion. The cool river and the shading gums seemed very attractive.

'We've got to help out here,' my father said. 'For a few days at least. We can't leave people in such a mess.'

'Gillian would be rapt in seeing the place.' I said.

'Of course she can come,' my mother agreed.

'No,' I said. 'She'd like to be invited.' I disliked my mother's mildly patronising tone, as if she allowed people to do things.

'Quite a few people have left already,' my mother said.

Looking around the dining room I saw that Rachel and Hans were absent, their table not even set. My father sighed, taking a deep breath as he leaned back into his chair.

'She was very upset by the devastation,' he said. 'She

was quite alright during the fire. She behaved excellently. She helped other people, but when it was all over she broke down rather badly. It was the stench. Hans said it reminded her of the ash that lay across the assembly area of the camps.'

'They just had to leave,' my mother added. 'And I think we should too.'

'It needs a good storm to clear the ocean,' I said.

'This black dust will be blowing around for weeks,' my mother said.

For both of us at that moment comfort and pleasant surroundings were the most important considerations.

'A few more days,' my father said.

Having experienced the aftermath of countless fires, he was useful, decisive, and could produce the right words for those whose properties had been wiped out. Outside the family he had a gift for encouragement.

'I think you should offer your help,' he said to me. 'You know how much water needs to go on a burning stump. Most of the volunteers think once the flame is out that's it.'

I wasn't too enthused.

'Hell, you've only got to tell them that, tell them to pour it on.'

'Yes, but if they haven't done it before, they don't really know how much. Listen, there are forests of stumps out there and I want you to help. And it'll stop you mucking about with this ridiculous obsession of yours.'

'You really think it's ridiculous.'

'Ridiculous in that you can do nothing about it.'

I couldn't argue with that. The realisation was something of a relief. I could begin feeling like an ordinary person once again.

Heavy with a good lunch I walked down to the RSL hall with my parents. I asked half-a-dozen drivers if they needed help but they had plenty of volunteers, most of them young blokes who had missed out on the flame and were prepared to make do with the smoke. They were still excited by the prospect of cleaning up. They would have volunteered for a war to satisfy their desire to be involved. It seemed to me as if all interests of the human race were somehow running parallel. It wasn't the judge's collection versus Larra's. It was an identical interest, and Larra's imagination couldn't quite take him into the class of the judge. Or could it? Had it simply come adrift and he wanted to anchor his dreams to some reality?

The trucks roared out from the parking area, bouncing over the gutter to the road. The volunteers hung onto the railings, grinning at one another, bewildered by the strange sensations; a taste of exhilaration at last.

Eventually I got a lift in a ute that needed operators for half-a-dozen back sprays. They were going out to the old scout camp where there were a few buildings apparently still smouldering and from where a few things could be saved. It was a wonder there hadn't been a truck out before this. In most emergencies, the rule is usually, save the institutions first.

There were a couple of other blokes and two girls in the back. They were taking their involvement very seriously, making sure they knew exactly how the sprays worked; clearly they would have liked to don them right there in the ute despite the bumping. But it was ridiculous that I should take such a superior attitude.

The two girls, wary of being thrown out of the back when the next man came along, were examining the long brass nozzles as though intimate knowledge would be required the moment they descended from the ute. It was no different from my days in the cadet units at school when finally, after weeks of waiting, we were allowed to handle real rifles. The two boys were smirking and nudging one another when they realised that I wasn't going to join in their bullshitting, they began to sneer challenges: who did I think I was? I turned to look at the stricken country. One of the blokes pushed me with his foot.

'What are you on about?' he said.

'Nothing,' I answered, 'So knock it off.'

After a few minutes silence he said, 'You're a bit on yourself aren't you?'

I looked out for a moment at the blackened countryside, then turned to him and began laughing. The sound was humorous but I could feel the tears beginning to turn my eyes hot.

'You stupid bastard,' I said. 'Look at this. Don't you know what that is?'

'I don't think you should speak like that in front of the girls,' the dead bastard said.

It was the refuge of the ignorant and the hypocritical. They knew perfectly well that most people used this langauge, theirs, including girls. But before replying, I looked across at the two girls and decided that my reply was in fact unspeakable in their presence.

'Can it,' I said, 'unless you want to get into it.'

'Huh,' he said contemptuously, and that satisfied him.

The track to the camp had been covered in heavy foliage. Now we drove through a scenery of smoking matchsticks. The ocean in the distance was a sparkling blue with an ash foreground. The scouts could have run to the water from here. It was only a thirty yard drop from the sheer cliffs. We came to where the first camp bungalows had been. Several silhouetted skeletons were all that remained of the buildings. Nothing salvable. As we crossed the creek however, the driver spotted smoking bridge supports and asked one of us to go and check them. I jumped over the side of the ute and one of the girls handed me a back spray.

'We'll go on further,' the driver said. 'Be an hour at the most.'

I slung on the back pack, the handle of the hydraulic pump protruding on the right side about waist level. The bastard was heavy especially for walking in water. The creek was so black, I couldn't judge its depth. It reflected the sky and then me descending. A summer creek wouldn't be deep, I thought. But still unsure, I left the pack swung on only one shoulder.

The warm sludge of the creek reached me before I faced the bridge. The structure had been burning for so long that the joints had parted and they could no longer feed flame to each other. I began pumping, adjusting the nozzle to probe the smouldering timber. It was a neat little bridge, or had been, probably built by the scouts themselves. Over to the right was a blackened corrugated iron shed that I hadn't noticed before. Leading up to it were the tracks of a motorcycle, black in the grey ash. I ignored them to concentrate on getting a steady stream of water into a joint where small flames danced when a breeze drifted down the creek bed. I decided that the bridge would be too dangerous a job for kids. The top support of the bridge was only two yards above the water, and then there was some heavy scaffolding shoring up the sides of packed earth. The only way to save it would involve dragging through a concrete pipe and letting the earth collapse around it. It all seemed too much for me; I thought I'd give the effort away. Besides, even if the timber supports kept smouldering, there was no risk of fire spreading. But I wasn't thinking things through properly. If I could extinguish the smouldering, the bridge would keep the creek clear until it could be replaced; otherwise with the amount of dirt falling, the creek could even change course. Fuck it. After the recent extreme situations during the fire, I was not coping with ordinary, practical problems.

A shadow cut the sun and I glanced up.

'You little shit,' Larra said.

He swung down hard with a chopping heel on a support. It gave instantly, a puff of sparks lighting the air for a moment. I turned to run but the water around my waist held me in slow motion. And the knapsack, heavy with water, was more than I could cope with. I twisted back so that my head would have a chance to stay at the surface. The falling timber collapsed as slowly as scaffolding peeling from a building. The first cross beam pinned my legs, forcing them into the mud. The next beam caught me across the chest, more like a heavy door closing on me, than a painful wallop. My body recalled to me instantly that I had been in a similar position: in a massive breaking wave, where you relax, don't fight it, and then drop through the turmoil of water to the bottom. The timber supports of this section locked themselves against either side of my body. My eyes hurt as I tried to see through the dirty water. It was brown which meant I wasn't far from the surface, but although my back wasn't against the mud my legs were effectively clamped. I tried to twist, knowing that if I showed the slightest sign of life above the water Larra would descend and kill me.

I heard thumping sounds and knew he was attempting to move the packed earth exposed by the scaffolding. I visualised him as a demented creature on a pogo stick. He must have realised he wasn't achieving much because the sound stopped. Terrified, I imagined him coming along the bank to find me.

I was beginning to feel the tension of my body. I could last four minutes without a breath but that was under relaxed circumstances. I had no idea how much time was passing. I became aware that I was still holding the brass nozzle of the end of the hose from the knapsack. The bulky bloody thing might be responsible for my position but it might also just help me. I wished I had played with the nozzle the way the girls had, but it unscrewed instantly. Someone had had the sense to clean the equipment. I moved carefully, hoping there would be no tell-tale swirls above me. The nozzle reached the six inches to the surface and I cleared the water from it with a quick blow. I wasn't sure how long I lay there sucking brass, but there were no obvious sounds of Larra. I thought that I could wait until the truck returned but that was panicky stuff. I risked pushing my legs back and forth in the mud, hoping the action wouldn't lower the beam onto my chest. It was easier than I had thought and I slipped my shoulders from the knapsack before surfacing tentatively. My eyes were stinging badly but I could see that Larra wasn't around. I crawled up the bank, my shins barked and bloodied. The realisation of my vulnerability was terrifying. Peeping over the bank I focussed on the tracks crossing the ash to the shed. I had almost decided to run, but I knew that it would have meant walking out on the Larra scene for the rest of my life.

A metallic ringing echoed from the shed. Larra was stripping heavy machinery, obeying a code of the bush which says knock off anything that moves and anything that doesn't. With the sounds vibrating in my ears I sprinted across the ash. I began praying — a most unusual event — that the sounds wouldn't stop.

At the shed I crept around the back and ducked beneath the only window cut into the corrugated iron. The clear ringing sounds stopped and I crouched motionless. Above me a hand appeared suddenly on the sharp sill, resting casually. Then I heard the steady beat of fluid on iron, a mockery of falling rain. The bastard was leaning there calmly, his fly open, taking a leak. The ludicrous situation helped me to transcend fear. I straightened with a grip around the brass nozzle but the pain was excruciating. I heard my voice saying, 'Shit, oh shit,' and in a movement intended to relieve pain, I jumped towards the shed entrance. Larra emerged looking for me, still shaking his head, and I struck him with a backhanded blow on the nape of the neck. As if in a nightmare, I watched him go down and then begin to rise again immediately. I felt like a fighter who had felled a powerful opponent with a lucky blow but the bastard was beating the ten count. While he was on his hands and knees I took a running kick at his head. My wet desert boots seemed powerless. I kicked him in the head several more times and then crunched him with a rabbit killer from my foot. The wet boots just seemed to splat on him, with little more effect than the sound.

He was obviously woozy but my efforts weren't exactly taking him to a lower level of consciousness. I was becoming weak with the concentrated effort. I remembered as a kid killing a frill-necked lizard. Everytime I had hit it with a piece of brick it had turned to face me with its bloodied mouth open. Halfway through that work I wished I had never started. One of Larra's eyes now seemed to be focussing on me. I needed a decent weapon to turn the bastard into a carcass. I kicked him hard in the side of the chest and then pushed him over with my foot. He slumped, unable to maintain the slightest balance. I grabbed his head. It was slippery but the hair gave a handhold. I inserted the small knob of the nozzle in Larra's ear.

'You're going around the world you bastard,' I said as I drove it home with my knee.

He convulsed quickly and his legs began a spasmodic shaking like an animal shot in the head.

Inside the shed was a tractor and Larra's old khaki motorbike. The beams were blackened but the entrance to the shed had been facing away from the flames so the interior had hardly been damaged. It was difficult to imagine the freak circumstance that had saved it from the incineration that had caught everything else.

Further inside was a four gallon can of petrol. I pulled Larra in beside the tractor and covered him with sloshes of petrol, pouring it in his ear. Then I ran to find some smouldering wood. As I ran back the draught fanned the flame. I tossed it in the door. The explosion knocked me to the ground and pieces of corrugated iron flew high over me. The violence astonished me. Inside was an inferno.

I walked back to the bridge, watching the flames burn themselves down in what was left of the shed. Gradually, inside my ribs I felt the structure of triumph being built. It developed into a warmth, prickling up my back in the way fear sometimes spreads. I leapt in the air and yelled 'Yaaaaah Yaaaaah' to the sky.

It was like a new beginning. My past could no longer cripple me. I had killed, demolished, destroyed, and a renewal process was beginning. I could be anything. It seemed I had killed my lion. I was stopped then by the thought that killing could exhilarate. Were leaders motivated by that? Were ordinary people? Could world leaders expunge their failures by a decision to take their countries to war, thus vicariously cleansing themselves with the news of successful battles? Shit.

The ute turned up half-an-hour later. The driver asked me if I had heard an explosion. I didn't answer immediately. I pointed to the smoking structure, now not looking any different from the rest of the landscape.

'It went while I was down the creek. It must have had fuel there.'

It would be weeks before Larra was discovered.

After a few other small jobs the ute headed back to town. Trucks were lined up at the town's water. Like an elephant's swaying trunk, the huge canvas feeder swung from the pipe that supported it. When one truck pulled from under it, it bounced there in the headlights of another, dripping litres, despite being turned off, until the next truck was properly stationed.

I told the ute driver I had to get going. 'See ya,' said a couple of voices.

It might have been that I had done nothing at all. I was calm, self-posessed even, and there was a pleasant lightness to my body despite the filthy clothes. Nevertheless, I found myself wondering whether I shouldn't walk back to the guest house by a longer path, in order to give myself time to think. It was the last thought I was aware of until that route had been traversed, and I had absolutely no memory of it.

When I reached the guest house I thought I should walk around the block, but the next thing I was aware of was of being back at the house, unsure as to whether I had made the trip or not. Time was behaving in a most peculiar way. I thought of the beach, my great balm for many problems. Now, walking through the sand dunes, my thoughts began to clear. I had been reliving the triumph of the killing, secretly massaging my ego, puffing at it. And what had I been creating? Fuel for future needs? Perhaps nothing more than that. Or was I in fact fuelling a desire for the recurrence of similiar circumstances? A mortifying guilt caught me then; I stood amongst the skeleton ti-trees, completely uncertain as to what I should do.

I trudged up the balding ridge of sand dunes. From there I looked out over the ocean, where blue had become a dominant colour again about a mile out. Then I turned and looked across the ravaged town, the wasted foothills and the blackened swathes cut into the ranges. That bastard was responsible for all this I thought. Without him there'd be some young kids still alive and some parents able to be happy, and I wouldn't have known the cowardice of men and been vulnerable to it myself. He had imagined he had dispensed with me, and without thinking further, had immediately gone about his larcenous work. In fact his greed to get back to business might have saved my life. Yeah, I thought, all that's right. But what about my enjoyment? I knew I would have to hide that. I wouldn't even be able to broach the subject with Gillian because her perception and sensitivity in discussions would leave me open to discovery. And a discovery of that nature about a person is not to be tolerated.

I was back on the guest house verandah and the speed of my change of location left me slightly disoriented. My father was being thanked by the proprietor for his work in saving the house. I passed by quickly, knowing that right now I wouldn't be able to look him in the eye. At the end of the hall the judge was talking to his wife Sarah through the open door of their room. I had an unbearable urge to tell him about my battle. It would be alright I told myself. It was an attack on me that had prompted my assault on Larra. I hesitated and turned into my room. There was no evidence that I had been attacked and there was no evidence that Larra had started the fires.

In my room I began to sweat, and my teeth started chattering. Alright, I told myself it's shock. Nothing to worry about; I'm not going to let it close down any functions. Dispense with those feelings of foreboding; they're not real. It would be stupid to give into them. Dangerous even. For a moment I believed I had left the nozzle protruding from the skull, Jesus, I thought, I'm a goner. Why did I do that? Why didn't I think? And then I remembered having rubbed it clean in the creek water, connected it, and pumped pressure through to free collected tissue. Shaky, I lay on the floor, my feet resting on the end of the bed. Come on, come on, what do other people feel? How do they continue to survive? I knew from the returned soldiers' stories that those in the front line could often become flip about death, concealing it until they were a few beers over their limit. Once they and their mates were boozed enough, there was no true listening or remembering.

And a judge? What's his first thought for the day when he wakes after pronouncing a death sentence? Does he ever wake knowing he's wrong and suffer despair for the loss of *his* innocence? It would need a strong belief in the law to be able to use it as an instrument of death. Procedure could allow him to wash his hands of a sentence. Procedure says that a judge must pronounce the death sentence if a jury finds an individual guilty of murder. But a judge doesn't have to step close to a cold neck, place a rope around it, watch and work the instrument that physically kills the victim. He escapes guilt because he only kills the person with words and procedures in his court. It occurred to me that the Nazi judges had used the same escape mechanism.

We're all bastards, I thought. Fuck it, I'm not going under if no one else does. And then I wondered whether that thought had sprung from strength or weakness? At the moment I didn't care. It was good that I didn't have to nail myself to any cross. I was innocent. Well not entirely, as my fantasies of killing Larra were proof enough of my intentions. But, I reasoned, I had acted out of fear. It had been a matter of attack or die. A judge doesn't impose death sentences out of fear. For him it wasn't a question of attack or die.

Slowly my frantic heart subsided. I saw that I could be innocent in my own right. I didn't need the approval or the rationalisation of others. An overwhelming sense of relief followed.

When I woke I lay stiff and uncomfortable, my mind clear of impressions. Then the doubt entered my consciousness. My body responded in a panicky way before my mind remembered. Christ, I thought, it was alright being philosophical about it. But the reality was that not only had I broken the law, but in the worst possible way. I should admit to it and sort it out with the authorities. We had been taught that to kill someone was an irretrievable step, that the guilt would always be there to dog your footsteps, unless the wound could be cauterised so completely that it would disappear. At first I thought that I could assume the mask of trauma. But such a radical reaction would be like placing a wonky lid on a garbage bin, something nasty would emerge. I also saw that to adopt other people's rationalisations was simply to apply another lid. The whole damn thing was my responsibility, and I had to use a muckrake to enable me to face the worst in myself. Meanwhile I had to walk from the room and face others.

Later I walked on the beach with Gillian. Not the blackened beach, but beyond, where the sand curved white in a welcoming smile. I listened to the grunt of dumping waves distorted by an irregular wind.

'I killed him you know,' I said abruptly.

Gillian twisted quickly towards me, her hair flying.

'What are you talking about?'

'The bastard tried to kill me.'

'But you were looking for him,'

'I was before. But not this time.'

She was silent as we walked along the beach, the water was a gleaming black mirror sliding up to us. I looked at her a couple of times but she didn't respond. Her face was calm in profile.

'Are you going to be caught?' she asked. It was my turn for silence.

'I don't think so,' I said eventually.

'It wasn't your fault?'

'No.'

'Well you can tell the police,' she said.

'I don't want to,' I said.

'Have you got any choice?'

'Yes,' I said. 'He was burnt up.'

Another description began to occur to me.

'Tenderised, skewered and sizzled,' I said. 'The bastard deserved all he got.'

I began to giggle, and then was close to tears.

The human performance suddenly seemed so frightful. The first person to kill an animal might have been disturbed by the terminating of such beauty. The first time the Nazis placed the Jews in the gas chambers they may have had some qualms. But what the hell, it was soon over and you were at home playing with your youngsters, all the while tolerating the horrors you were foisting on other families. And the law was being obeyed.

'Can you live with what you have done?' Gillian asked.

'Yes,' I said. 'I was trying to save my own life.'

'It seems you did more than that,' she said. 'Skewered and sizzled sounds like you enjoyed it.'

'Yes,' I said. 'It does sound like that. I think I was just relishing the moment of surviving myself.'

At the end of the beach we stopped to examine the clear, still rock pools. Close up we saw the skidding life above and below the surface. I began to speculate about the reasons for the motion. An innocuous enough pastime. The first curious creatures must have thought so too. But now it seemed to me that over those hundreds of thousands of years of study we had reached the worst conclusions. Did each individual always have to begin at the beginning? Surely there must exist the possibility of a memory passed on from generation to generation in a less hit and miss way?

Robert Drewe
**The Bodysurfers**

A collection of short stories set against the familiar sensual background of the Australian beach — and occurring over three generations of the middle-class Lang Family. This sophisticated, compelling and blackly humorous book uses the basic coastal elements of climate, ocean, leisure and the pursuit of serenity to express the age-old themes of sexual and familial love, jealousy, escape, despair and survival.

'a remarkably seductive and exuberant collection which manages, in its portrayal of human relationships, to be both mordant in tone and playful in manner' THE TIMES LITERARY SUPPLEMENT

'…a brilliant book. It is clever, touching and at times desperately funny.' CANBERRA TIMES

'Robert Drewe's stories are always accurate and sensitive, often comic, at moments brilliant' SYDNEY MORNING HERALD

'The surf and its followers are the unbreakable link, smelling of salt, glistening with suntan oil, somnolent with sex, all embraced in affectionate prose, measuring out life along the coast to which Australians always run.' THE SUN HERALD

Tim Winton
**An Open Swimmer**

An Australian/Vogel Award
Winning Novel

Jerra Nilsam and his old schoolfriend Sean are on a fishing trip on the wild and beautiful West Australian coast. Sean has completed university and has a respectable job. Jerra is a dreamer, searching for the fish that holds a pearl...

A carefully woven pattern of dialogue, dreams and memories gradually disclose the true nature of Jerra's past—his relationships with his family, with Sean and with Sean's mother, Jewel. Together with the richness of accumulated images, it works to provide the story of a young man's inner development with a structure and texture that is impressively original.

'...exciting and original—a masterpiece of concise, vivid writing...' SUNDAY INDEPENDENT

'With a gentle, intricate pattern of symbol and remembrance, Winton links Jerra's delight in fishing and the underwater world with brooding images of mutilation and guilt, with awakening sexuality, with the loss of innocence and displacement of ideals. Sharp-edged scenes break through on beaches, underwater, by campfires, on city streets and on the rocky terrain of Jerra's past.' THE AGE

'beautifully written' THE WEST AUSTRALIAN